MORLEY LIBRARY

3 0112 1042 6552 2

W9-AIA-151

PINOT ENVY

EDWARD FINSTEIN

Copyright 2013 Edward Finstein.
All rights reserved.

No part of this book may be reproduced in any form or by electronic means,
including information storage and retrieval systems, without written permission
from the publisher, except by a reviewer, who may quote passages in a review.

Cover Design: Steve Parke
Interior Design: Tracy Copes
Author Photo: Ravenshoe Group

Published by Bancroft Press
"Books that Enlighten"
800-637-7377
P.O. Box 65360, Baltimore, MD 21209
410-764-1967 (fax)
www.bancroftpress.com

ISBN 978-1-61088-089-3
Printed in the United States of America

To Pooky, whose love, support, strength, and
inspiration continually guide me and
make me a better person

CHAPTER 1

Holy mother of pearl! I couldn't believe my eyes. What the hell were *they* doing here?

Kneeling on an incline up against a chain-link fence, not far from its entrance, I shifted my binocs from hand to face as they examined the open storage unit. It was evening, and from maybe 210 feet away, my view was not great, especially when the light was not exactly shining over the unit in question. The ground under my feet was damp and slippery from the rain that had fallen an hour or two earlier. I was surrounded by a small oak tree, high grass, weeds, cedars, and lilac bushes. It was unusually warm for the time of year, and a decent wind was blowing. The air was filled with the combined fragrant scent of blooming lilacs, dank earth, and my own sweat.

The constant buzzing of a beehive not far away kept me on edge. A lone woodpecker in the oak above tapped on the tree, beating out a rhythm that strangely echoed my rapid heartbeat. I was both anxious and nervous.

I hate stakeouts.

My targets began to move away from the facility, and my line of vision was blocked by some of the units, so I started to make my way out to follow the action. I knew they weren't very far off at this point, because I could still hear them talking as they opened their car doors.

But as I exited my position and ran in their direction, I slipped on the incline and fell down onto the roadside. It felt like I'd sprained my ankle. As I straightened myself up, a motor suddenly came to life. Highlighted by the car's headlamps, I knew I had been made. I feared some sort of retaliation, but the car whizzed right by me. The folks within were the same two I'd watched by the storage unit.

Bewildered, confused, and breathing hard, I hobbled back to my car as best I could. I sat there, trying to regain my composure. I was scared and still sweating, and my ankle hurt from the fall. But after a while, I felt more together, and I put my wheels in gear and headed home.

As I motored along, I had the eerie feeling I was being followed. Checking my rear-view mirror, I spotted two guys in a maroon-colored Pontiac who seemed to be tailing me. This was not the car that had whizzed by me before. Just to be sure it wasn't my imagination, I changed lanes. They followed suit. I changed back. Ditto!

"Oh crap!" I squealed, slamming my hand into the steering column.

So I zigged—and so did my pursuer. Then I zagged—same deal.

Uh-oh, I thought. *Something is definitely rotten in the state of Denmark!*

Now, I'm normally a very careful driver, but this scenario gave me the willies, so I sped up, struggling to shake the tail. Weaving in and out of traffic, I almost sideswiped some guy, who responded by flipping me the bird. My heart was racing, and the sweats were back. As I came up behind some Sunday driver, there was nowhere else for me to go, so I leaned on the horn until the driver got the message and moved aside. Putting my foot to the metal so hard my back tires spun and smoked, I raced forward, a few times driving on the shoulder and kicking up dirt just to stay ahead. But through all of this, the pursuers kept pace.

I wanted to grab my cell phone to call the cops, but I couldn't risk taking my hands off the wheel.

As I crossed the Bay Bridge, I thought for a moment that I had lost them, but damn, there they were again, a few car lengths back in the lane next to mine. My ankle was throbbing and my shirt was soaked. Once back in San Francisco, I zoomed up and down side streets to lose them, but it was even harder here with pedestrian traffic and parked cars.

"Get the hell out of the way!" I screamed at some kids playing ball in the street.

I had to swerve onto the sidewalk to avoid a dog and an old lady. Still, they followed. *Where are the cops when you need them?* I thought.

My pursuers pulled right up against my back fender, and I could see their faces clearly. They were mean-looking dudes, and I could have sworn I'd seen them before. I'm sure they could smell my fear.

But then—a bit of luck! Spotting a garbage truck pulling away from the curb, I managed to speed up just enough to zip past it, and the truck intercepted my tail's pursuit.

Then I zoomed down another side street and parked on an alley not too far from home. I sat there panting like a dog just back from a run in the middle of summer. Waiting about five minutes, which seemed like an eternity, I saw no sign of them. I had lost them. I breathed a sigh of relief, then drove very, very cautiously home, all the while checking my rear-view mirror, waiting for my heart to return to normal.

Parking in my driveway, I proceeded to the front door.

All of a sudden, I felt myself grabbed from behind. I couldn't see my attacker. I tried to turn to get a look at whoever it was, but took a heavy blow to the face.

That's the last thing I remember.

CHAPTER 2

I t had all started about a month ago, back in early June, after a morning spent doing my thing in the wine biz. I had taught a wine appreciation class at Rosewell College, where I've been on-faculty for the last eight years, and lunched with a potential client who wanted me to appraise his wine cellar. The rest of the afternoon was devoted to writing—a column for one of my regular gigs in *Haute Living*, a lifestyle magazine, and some preliminary notes on a new wine book idea I was developing, a follow-up to my last award-winning publication, *Wine is a Four-Letter Word*.

I work out of my three-bedroom bungalow in the North Beach part of San Francisco, where I live with Mouton, my four-year-old, longhaired, tortoiseshell cat. I found her as a stray kitten in a back alley outside Albona, a local restaurant, next to some empty wine bottles, one of which was a Mouton Rothschild. I named her after the wine.

By eight that night, I was with my two favorite people, my Aunt Sadie and my girlfriend, Julia Harper, in the living room of Sadie's nicely appointed, Asian-inspired apartment in elegant Pacific Heights, listening to an old CD recording of the 1930s *Shadow* radio show. As Sadie got up to make coffee, Julia was on my case again.

"Woody, I'm not going to hang around forever," she said. "You've been putting me off for a year."

"It'll happen, hon," I said. "I just need a little more time."

"Look, buster, my lease is coming up in the next month and a half. I really do not want to renew it."

As of late, Julia had been pressuring the hell out of me to take the next step in our relationship and let her move in with me. Julia and I had met about four years earlier when I did some consulting for her company—the Wine Emporium, the largest retailer of wine in America—and we'd been seeing each other the last two. Her blue eyes and flaming mane of red hair, which hung down almost to her waist, attested to her Belfast, Ireland origins, where she had lived until the age of twelve. At thirty-one, she was not what I would call beautiful, but there was something about her—an incredibly appealing inner passion. She always knew exactly what she wanted, when she wanted it. That sometimes created turmoil.

It's not that I didn't care for her enough to live with her. I believed I loved her. Maybe I was nervous, because all the man/woman live-in relationships I saw growing up never seemed to work. My own mother and father fought like cats and dogs. Maybe I didn't trust myself. I still enjoyed looking at beautiful women and admit being tempted at times, but I'd always been faithful.

When Sadie returned with the coffee, Julia excused herself to visit the powder room.

"I heard you two going at it again," Sadie said, putting sugar in her cup.

"I know. It's making me crazy."

"You're going to lose her if you don't move in together. Do you want that?"

"No," I said. "We'll work it out."

Sadie is my mother's younger sister—worldly, larger-than-life, widowed. At sixty-three, blonde and blue-eyed, she's in great shape, dresses impeccably, and still turns heads. My uncle Moe had died four years earlier from cancer, and although he left her reasonably well off, poor investments and the recent recession had depleted her finances. Recently diagnosed with osteoporosis, Sadie had injured her hip, requiring an operation to replace it. She was in a fair bit of pain most of the time, and though she rarely complained about it, I knew she had let her health insurance lapse.

She and I had always been close. As long as I can remember, my mother was not a well woman, bedridden much of the time, and my upbringing would have been lacking big-time were it not for kind Sadie. She stepped in and taught me not only right from wrong, but also theater, music, arts, and fashion, especially from the 1930s to the 1950s. To this day, I love everything about the era: vaudeville, slapstick comedy, big band music, art deco, radio shows, and especially the clothes, like wide-lapelled suits and pleated pants. Although only thirty-five, I believe I was born decades too late.

I was never close with my rabbi father. My mother finally passed away when I was eighteen. Although I was devastated, I felt I had another mother waiting in the wings.

"I want you to be happy," Sadie said now. "I think moving in together is a good idea. You're not getting any younger yourself, you know."

At five foot eleven, with wavy brown hair, green eyes, and an average build, I was in pretty good shape. However, on my clean-shaven kisser, I could see some age lines starting to form around my eyes.

I was about to respond to Sadie when my phone rang. As Julia returned from the bathroom, and as she and Sadie settled back into listening to *The Shadow*, I stepped out into the hallway.

"Hi, Woody," said the voice on the other end. "Walter Pendry here. Did I get you at a bad time?"

"No, no, that's fine, Walter. What can I do for you?"

I knew Pendry from the University of California at Davis, where he was a professor of vinous history. He and I had worked together previously through the university's continuing education division. We co-hosted a series of seminars on the development of wine through the ages and how its taste had changed. UC Davis has a reputation as one of the finest schools in the northern hemisphere for winemaking and viticulture. Many of California's best winemakers and grape-growers are graduates.

"Listen, Woody, can you possibly come by my office at your earliest convenience? There's something absolutely incredible I have to talk to you about," he said.

"Can't you tell me about it over the phone?"

"Sorry, no can do! This could very well turn the world of historical wine on its head," he said, sounding very excited.

"And you're calling me because—"

"Because I think you can help. Look, you won't be disappointed," he said.

My interest piqued, we made an appointment for eleven the next morning. Once I hung up, I pondered what could possibly so affect the world of historical wine. I knew Pendry well enough to know he wouldn't waste my time if it wasn't something huge.

Turning my attention back to the ladies, I found Sadie had dozed off and was softly snoring. Julia was leafing through a fashion magazine. I lowered the volume on the CD player and went back to *The Shadow*.

CHAPTER 3

The next morning at about quarter to ten, I headed out to UC Davis, located off Highway 80, east of Napa Valley, southwest of Sacramento. Traffic was light, so I made good time.

My role in the wine business was usually consulting to restaurants and hotels, creating wine lists, training staff, and conducting tastings, but the focus had evolved further. A few years ago, I'd been caught up in a fraud situation regarding many vintages of a high-end, rare Amarone. My keen interest in antiques, especially rare vinous artifacts, had helped me solve the case, leading to other investigatory jobs. More and more, this had become a large part of what I do.

And I had a feeling Pendry hadn't called me up for a consultation.

I joined him just outside his office on campus. He was a distinguished chap in his late forties, about six feet tall with fine, straight black hair, a full beard bordering on gray, piercing blue eyes, and a congenial personality. Looking every bit the part of the professor, he was dressed in gray slacks, a white shirt, and a brown, suede-elbowed, tweed sport jacket.

(I always notice what people are wearing because, in investigatory work, how a person is dressed can often tell me something about their behavior. The fact that I'm a clotheshorse myself certainly doesn't hurt.)

Looking me up and down and shaking his head, he showed me into his office. It was so small you could hardly move in there. Books and documents were piled everywhere. I believe the term is "organized chaos"—*organized*, because I'd bet he knew exactly where everything was.

"Would you like a coffee?" he said, turning his answering machine on so he could receive messages and not have to answer the phone directly.

"Sure," I said, looking around.

"Espresso okay?"

"Great," I said, surprised he could find a spot for anything else in this cubbyhole.

He went to one corner of the room and flung a few documents aside to reveal a small espresso-maker. As he worked, I took the only other chair besides his and looked at all the degrees and accolades on his walls. Truly a well-respected man of education and science!

Finally, with the day's first cup of java in hand, I asked what this was all about.

"Are you familiar with French history—specifically, that of Napoleon Bonaparte?" said Pendry.

"I know Napoleon became a military commander at a very young age and married an older woman, Josephine, who only married him so she wouldn't be destitute. In fact, she was quite the hotsy-totsy."

Pendry looked at me funny. "Geez, my dad uses that expression," he said. "Did you know Napoleon was a wine lover?"

"Of course! Being French, you'd expect as much. I believe the general had his own supply of the dessert wine, vin de Constance, from South Africa. If the theory of death by poisoning is correct, that wine may have been the way they bumped him off."

"In fact, Pinot Noir from the prized Grand Cru Le Chambertin of Burgundy's Côte-d'Or was his favorite."

"Really? I didn't know that. He had good taste," I said, taking a sip of my espresso.

Pendry informed me that Napoleon often had barrels with him on his campaigns and was quoted many times as saying, "Nothing makes the future so rosy as to contemplate it through a glass of Chambertin."

"However, the little guy was obviously a peasant," said Pendry, "'cause he always mixed the vino with ice."

"With ice? How blasphemous! No wonder they exiled him to Elba."

When Napoleon married Josephine in 1796, Pendry told me, he had a number of bottles from the spectacular 1784 vintage etched with his initials—somewhat akin to what Thomas Jefferson did with the bottles of 1787 Lafite he had produced in France when he was George Washington's personal wine advisor.

"So who was the producer of Napoleon's red pop?" I said.

"That's the thing," Pendry said. "Napoleon asked that the bottle labels display only his own coat of arms and not the producer's name. Could be anyone, but chances are it's one of the older houses, like Latour."

"That's all fascinating, Professor," I said, sitting back in my chair, "but what's the point here?"

"All the bottles were consumed at some point," said Pendry, "except for one—a double magnum." That would comprise three thousand milliliters of wine in one very large bottle.

"What happened to it?"

Pendry got up, stuck his head out into the hall, and looked once in each direction before closing the door.

"Up until recently," he said, "it was thought to be owned by a French corporation in Avignon, France. But as it turns out, it was purchased by someone else about a year ago—a wealthy grape-grower right here in northern California. Very few know about it."

"It must be worth a fortune."

"This double magnum with Napoleon's initials is estimated in today's market to be worth approximately $2.5 million."

"Christopher Columbus, that's a lot of coin!" I said, trying to imagine that kind of cash. "The present owner must keep that bottle locked away in Fort Knox."

"He had a special, temperature-controlled vault built for it on his property just outside downtown Napa," said Pendry. "The security surrounding it was tighter than whatever's holding Donald Trump's hair in place."

"You said *was*," I said, looking at him curiously.

That's how I learned why Pendry had called me here. The bottle had been stolen.

"Has he contacted the police?" I said.

"No, he doesn't want the authorities involved," Pendry said. "Only a few people know of the wine's existence, and that's the way he'd like to keep it."

When I asked how I could help, Pendry said, "The owner is willing to pay quite handsomely for the Pinot's safe return."

When I asked why he didn't just have this chap contact me directly, he said that the guy was very particular about who took on the case. He wanted Pendry to screen candidates in advance.

I was quite busy with teaching, writing my columns, a potential appraisal, and the new book, but I figured it couldn't hurt to at least meet with the richnik and see where that took me.

"One last thing," I said. "Is this guy a wine lover, or is his interest in rare vintages merely for investment purposes?"

"What difference could that possibly make?" Pendry said, writing down his address on a piece of paper.

"Oh, I don't know. Just curious, I guess."

I was lying. If the truth be known, it made a world of difference to me, at least on an ethical level. My years in the wine biz had taught me that there are numerous kinds of wine lovers out there. Those with little money buy what they can afford and enjoy it immensely. Those with more money buy better wine and enjoy it substantially. Those with gobs of money fall into two categories. One buys high-end product and enjoys drinking it as much as collecting it—a true wine lover taking full advantage of personal wealth. The other buys and collects wine merely for prestige, often purchasing labels rather than wine. It's an expensive investment that impresses. These latter people, I really don't like to be involved with.

After studying at some of the best wine schools in the world in England, Australia, and here in California, I had managed to parlay my longtime love of *vino* into a pretty good life. I'd spent the last twelve years in the wine business because of my fascination with history—there's history in every bottle—and I'd found that most folks genuinely interested in wine were well-educated, reasonably intelligent people interested in travel, culture, the arts, and the gastronomic pleasures of life.

"Wait a minute," said Pendry. "You're not suggesting this guy is faking the whole thing just to defraud money from the insurance company? He's rich. Why would he?"

"Whoa. Hold on there, Walter. Where'd that come from? Been watching too many legal dramas on TV, have you? I'm not suggesting anything," I said, taking the piece of paper from him and stashing it in my pocket. "Just trying to understand his motivation!"

"Now you're an amateur shrink, are you?" He chuckled.

I had to admit, I *did* wonder if this guy was just hoping to make a bundle back on the insurance and reinvest it in something else, or if he was a sincerely, passionate wine lover treasuring a romantic bit of vinous *histoire*.

I was about to find out.

CHAPTER 4

J ames McCall lived just off Highway 29 in the Los Carneros area, a famous part of northern California wine country that actually straddles the south end of both Napa and Sonoma Valleys. The drive there from Davis took about twenty-five uneventful minutes.

Napa Valley, itself about an hour north of San Francisco, is world-famous as a premium wine-growing region, and boasts some of the most expensive real estate on the planet. A mere twenty miles long and five miles wide, it runs from the town of Calistoga in the north to just below the town of Napa in the south. Well over 250 wineries call it home, and with all the glitz and glam, it doesn't take long to realize there's tons of money tied up here.

Arriving at McCall's expansive estate, I announced myself through an intercom at the gate. It slowly opened, and I drove my canary yellow Corvette through. Motoring along for what seemed like an eternity past a small lake, stables with numerous horses, an orchard, gardens and, of course, tons of grapevines, I arrived high on a hill at a magnificent, plantation-style, whitewashed house, complete with columns.

For a moment, I imagined Rhett Butler scoffing at Scarlett. "Frankly, my dear, I don't give a damn," I muttered under my breath. But this moment passed when my attention landed outside the adjoining six-car garage. There, a gorgeous blonde in a baby-blue tank top and a pair of cut-offs that left little to the imagination busily polished a Mercedes sports coupe convertible. As I got out of my car, this vision hardly even gave me a sidelong glance, continuing instead to buff her car.

As I trudged up toward the house, the front door swung open. A short, somewhat stout lady somewhere between forty and death greeted me. With a slight Scandinavian accent, she introduced herself as Ms. Svenson, the housekeeper. It was the same voice I had spoken with through the intercom.

In the grand foyer, I nearly stopped dead in my tracks when I saw the same beauty who had been out polishing her car when I drove up. Now she was dressed in blue jeans and a cowboy shirt. *My God, that woman's a quick-change artist*, I thought. It couldn't have been any more than forty seconds since I'd last seen her.

Ms. Svenson led me down a long hallway and to the library, at which point she left, instructing me to wait for Mr. McCall. Although the architectural structure outside echoed *Gone with the Wind*, the interior of the house, here in the library in particular, smacked of neo-Classicism with a soupçon of Roman Gothic—a strange combination for sure, but somehow it seemed to work. The library was a two-story affair with a balcony, if you can believe it, and a spiral staircase right out of *My Fair Lady*.

While I waited, I studied the titles of the nearest books. Many were classics—in fact, opening a few, I discovered they were first editions. I was surprised—such literary gems are very valuable and usually kept under lock and key. One in particular, a leather-bound copy of Hemingway's *For Whom the Bell Tolls*, got my blood pumping. I picked it out and started to leaf through it.

"Ah, Hemingway!" came a strong voice from directly behind me. "Did you know he invested in a bar down in Key West just to help a friend pay the mortgage?"

Rather startled by the benign comment that came out of nowhere, I turned around to find a tall, good-looking man in his late fifties, maybe early sixties, with movie-star appeal. His silver-gray hair and perfect wax-tipped moustache decorated a face with piercing blue eyes.

"He also used to visit a little outdoor restaurant nearby," I said, deciding to play along, "to watch cockfights and boxing matches."

"Is that a fact?" The man stepped forward. "I'm James McCall."

"A pleasure to meet you, sir," I said, offering my hand and a business card.

As he looked me up and down, making a strange face, he took the card but didn't shake my hand.

"Woodrow," my host said, examining my card. "That's an unusual first name."

"My mother was a huge fan of President Woodrow Wilson. Unfortunately, she never really gave any thought to the consequences. Kids can be so cruel, ya know? Just call me Woody," I said.

"Have a seat," he said, directing me to a chair.

"You have some amazing books here, sir," I said, sitting down.

"There's a timelessness to the classics that modern storytellers like Grisham, Patterson, and Clancy just can't match. No graphic murders and sex—just damn good writing! Give me Dickens, Austen, and Hemingway every time."

"I couldn't agree more, sir."

"A drink, Mr. Robins?"

"Please call me Woody," I said. "And yes, thanks! I'm sure the sun is over the yardarm somewhere in the world."

"I just opened a 1985 La Tâche. That'll have to do."

I almost fell out of my seat. The 1985 La Tâche, a Grand Cru red Burgundy from an amazing year, was a spectacular wine. Although it was only early June, it was hotter outside than Paris Hilton's love life, and I'd have preferred something cool to drink, but one does not say no to a wine of such caliber.

McCall summoned Ms. Svenson, who immediately appeared with a tray, two Reidel Burgundy glasses, a decanter filled with the glorious nectar, and the empty bottle. As she placed the decanter down on a sideboard and poured a couple of glasses, I could tell from the way she handled the crystal that she had done this before.

Glasses in hand, we examined the brilliant liquid, made love to it with our olfactory senses, and sipped cautiously. Both of us chewed, gargled, and inhaled air as we imbibed. The only thing we didn't do was spit, but that would have been a crime with a wine this special. Full of stewed red fruit, cedar, earth, a silky supple mouth feel, and a finish longer than Cyd Charisse's legs, the wine was deliriously delicious.

"So, what do you think?" McCall said.

"Ain't nothing like the classics. Thank you."

"I do enjoy sharing my wine with someone who can appreciate it," he said. "Although I like all varietals and have a very eclectic collection, I'm absolutely mad about Pinot Noir. That's why I became a grape-grower. Clonal selection is so important, and Pinot's a pig to grow—hard as hell on the soil and best suited to temperate, foggy, even downright cold appellations. The longer the berries can hang on the vine before becoming too ripe, the more complex the wine, yet too much heat and sun causes it to ripen before it has a chance to develop its full potential. It's really tough to get right. They sure got it right with this '85 La Tâche, though."

He seemed almost crazed as his eyes glazed over. He knew his Pinot all right. If I'd had any doubts about his genuine passion for *vino* in general, and Pinot and Burgundy in particular, they were entirely put to rest.

"So tell me about the missing wine," I said, reaching into my briefcase and recovering a hand-held miniature tape recorder.

"Put that away," McCall demanded suddenly. "There'll be no recording here."

I was shocked. I was merely going to run it during our conversation about the wine so I wouldn't forget any of the details. Obeying his orders, though, I slipped the tape recorder back in my bag and sat back in my chair, glass in hand.

"The situation is most disturbing," he said. From here, he was all business.

About a week ago, he'd hosted a small dinner party for some family and close friends who were to stay the night. Just before retiring at about midnight, McCall checked—as he always did in the morning and before bed—the settings on the alarm system controlling the wine vault. The monitor of the security panel showed the wine in the vault, but the digital readout said the alarm had last been disarmed somewhere around half past nine that night. McCall quickly disarmed the system and entered the vault, only to find the wine gone.

"How could the monitor show the wine present when it wasn't there?" McCall said. "The system must have malfunctioned somehow."

"Did you mention the theft to any of your guests or staff?" I said, leaning forward in my chair.

"Just to Ms. Svenson and Ralph Wader, my attorney."

"And who at this dinner party knew about the wine, sir?" I shifted in my seat.

"Everyone!"

Pendry had said that only a few people knew of its existence, but McCall gave me a rundown of everyone who had been at the dinner party, and all of them knew: his sister, Patricia, and her husband, Horace Botner; a good friend, Sam Spezzo, his wife, Lucy, and their son, Johnny; his attorney, Ralph Wader, and his wife, Jane; and his twin daughters, Emily and Denise. "You probably saw Emily cleaning her car out front when you drove up," said McCall.

Twins, eh? Well, that explained the quick-change artist,

"What about the staff?" I said, crossing my legs.

Besides the housekeeper I'd already met, there was the manservant, cook, gardener, and chauffeur. When asked if any of his staff lived at the house, he said his housekeeper, manservant, and chef did. He told me where to find their rooms.

"Didn't your wife attend?"

"My wife passed away last year," he said, with absolutely no change of expression.

"I'm so very sorry," I said.

We sat there in a long uncomfortable silence before I spoke.

"Have you received any kind of ransom note?" I said, folding my arms.

"No. Nothing."

This was not surprising. Often, perps will wait a week or so to make the owner more desperate and more likely to pay up.

"I'll pay you handsomely for your time and cover all expenses," said McCall. "You can even stay here in the guest cottage on the property, if you like. It has its own small wine cellar. So?"

I gave it some thought. I was extremely intrigued by this old vintage and its history, but if I decided to take this on, staying over at the estate for any length of time was out of the question. That might jeopardize my objectivity. I'd rather drive back and forth to San Fran than feel obligated in some way.

"I'll put you on a retainer of five hundred dollars a day," McCall said. "I'll cover all your expenses. In fact, I'll even throw in a bonus of, say, one hundred thousand dollars should you help recover my wine."

It didn't take a degree in economics to figure that I could make a potential killing off this case, and most importantly, I could help Sadie get her much-needed operation. But one thing really bugged me, and I wondered if I could overcome it.

In his demeanor, lack of emotion, and abruptness, McCall reminded me so much of my father. My father, the rabbi, was extremely wired to the synagogue, so he never had much time for me. It was a good thing, because the man was a tyrant. He forced me to attend rabbinical school to follow in his footsteps, but a small misdemeanor changed all that. I was caught in my dorm room with a young lady in a rather compromising position and booted out. For some crazy reason, the fact that she was not of the Jewish persuasion seemed to carry more weight than the act itself. Go figure. *Mein papa* was appalled. He disowned me and never forgave me. He passed away four years ago.

I mulled things over while taking another sip of the La Tâche. *Damn, that's good. If any of the other wines here are at all like this welcome imbibe, a case like this could prove a very delicious layover.*

So I accepted the case but agreed to stay only the night. I asked McCall to tell his staff I would be around asking questions, but not to tell them why. As I took another sip of the wine, I silently wondered whether I was doing the right thing by saying yes.

CHAPTER 5

The first thing I had to do was take a look at the crime scene. McCall led me downstairs to the basement, where we walked up a long hallway, passing a home gym filled with Nautilus equipment, wet and dry saunas, and a laundry facility the size of my entire house. There were several major storage rooms, a furnace room, and a security control center.

Finally, we entered a large game room, which housed an antique pool table, an air-hockey table, a dart board, a shuffleboard unit, a couple of pinball machines, and a swank bar. The entire room was lined in deep mahogany paneling. On one wall was a solid wooden door McCall indicated led to his wine cellar.

"So that's where the Chambertin was kept?" I said, looking the door over.

"No, that's my regular wine cellar. It houses some 875 bottles."

"So where is the Chambertin vault? Professor Pendry said you had one specially built."

"What I'm about to show you must be kept strictly confidential. Do you understand?" said McCall, looking very secretive.

I nodded, of course. I didn't know why he was being so careful. After all, someone had obviously gotten in there—wherever *there* was—and pinched the wine.

He moved to the bar area and pushed down on one end of the counter. A square piece of the bar top flipped over, revealing a control panel with the small monitor he'd described earlier. I went over to examine it.

There were several keys below a digital display with a date and time. A slight residue of dust or something covered the keyboard and around the perimeter. *Don't they ever clean this?* I wondered. I wiped a little of the dust on my finger and put it up to my nose. It smelled like baby powder.

"Is there a baby in the house?" I said.

"What?" McCall barked.

"Never mind."

The monitor displayed the now-empty unit. I could see a foam mold in the shape of a large Burgundy bottle where the Chambertin must have laid on its side.

"You see the date and time here," McCall said, pointing at the console. "It shows May 30 as the last time the vault was opened, which was the night I discovered the wine missing."

"But where's the vault?" I said, looking around the room.

He pushed a series of numbers on the control panel. Suddenly, just to the right of the door to his main wine cellar, another door, completely camouflaged in the paneling, slowly swung open, a light switching on inside. *Holy moly!*

Inside was the same little chamber displayed on the monitor, approximately seven square feet, the empty unit in the center.

I stepped in and looked around. There was nothing else in the room, save a video camera mounted on the ceiling and a cooling unit I was sure kept the space at perfect cellar conditions. The floor was solid concrete and the walls appeared to be steel—two and a half feet thick on all sides, McCall informed me.

I stepped back out and examined the hidden door. It was steel of the same thickness, covered in paneling. Nothing about the security system looked the least bit suspicious.

"Okay, you can close it up now," I said.

McCall pushed the numbers again. The light went off, the door slowly closed, and once again the room was totally hidden. He pushed down on the countertop again and the square flipped back over. The bar surface looked completely normal.

I scanned the room for anything unusual but found nothing. When asked if anyone else knew the code to access the vault, he said no.

"I assume you had the system checked out by professionals to see if it was defective?"

"Yes," said McCall. "First thing the next morning, someone came out from Touchstone Security, the company that designed and installed the system, but they found nothing wrong."

"If someone was out here on May 31, did they not go into the vault?" I said, quite puzzled. The last date on the panel showed May 30.

"No, they didn't. I guess there was no reason to."

I must admit I found it a bit odd that the Touchstone Security person wouldn't check inside the penetrated vault. I asked McCall to contact another security company and have them come over and check out the system. He gave me a bit of an argument but ultimately agreed.

"When was the last time you were actually in the vault and saw the wine yourself?" I said.

"Several weeks before that night," McCall said. "I went in to adjust the camera angle, and the wine was definitely there."

"Do you have any security footage of this room?" I said, studying the space for a camera.

"I checked out all the footage from that entire day and found no evidence of anyone being down here."

"Now, you said that everyone who attended the dinner party that night knew you had the wine," I said. "Did they know where it was kept?"

"Yes."

Not too smart, I thought. Showing off the wine may have led to trouble.

"Do you have a photo of the wine, sir?"

"Yes, I'll give it to you upstairs."

As we headed back the way we had come, I asked if there was any other access down to the basement level. McCall informed me there wasn't.

As we reached the main level, Ms. Svenson appeared, announced that the cottage was ready, and handed me a key. She also gave me the code to bypass the security gates at the main entrance to the estate.

"Just follow the road past the garage, around the pond, and through the thicket of trees. You'll run right into it," she said.

"Is there Wi-Fi available in the cottage?" I said.

"Throughout the entire estate, sir," she replied.

"The photo, sir?" I said to McCall.

"Ah, yes, the photo! Hang on." He left me for a minute, then returned with an 8.5-by-11-inch color glossy. The bottle was sure impressive enough, made of smoky, grayish-green, hand-blown glass. Two-thirds of the way down the face of the bottle was the label. In its middle was Napoleon's coat of arms, blue and yellow with a knight's armored head surrounded by flowers and a fleur-de-lys. Beneath that, it simply said "Napoleon," and above it the words "*Viro constanti*." Above the label, the initials "NB" were etched into the glass.

Under the label, a second, smaller label said "Le Chambertin," and the vintage, 1784, was handwritten directly on the bottle with some sort of paint.

"Professor Pendry said he didn't know who the producer was. Do you?" I said.

"No, but bottling certain wines without the producer's name was apparently quite common back then among the aristocracy."

"All right, I think I have enough information to start," I said. "I'll have to search the entire house, of course, for other evidence and clues."

"Well, you won't be looking in my room," he said, quite firmly.

I was taken aback by his comment. "It would be rather sloppy of me to not look everywhere, you understand," I said.

"Absolutely not!" he said, glaring at me. "I don't like what you're implying."

"Sir, I'm not implying anything! I was just—"

He stopped me by holding up his hand and showing me the palm. I decided to let it ride, and as I started out the door, McCall called after me, "You'll be joining me on the patio at eight for dinner."

Thanks for asking if I'm available, I thought. The man was certainly used to command.

"It'll give you a good opportunity to meet my sister, her husband, and my daughters."

"Yes, sir. I'll be there," I said, somewhat ticked at his behavior.

As I returned to my car, I looked around for Blondie. She was nowhere in sight.

Now I really wondered if I was making a mistake in taking on this case. McCall was not exactly the warmest person in the world. He was totally serious, abrupt, a little obsessed—especially with Pinot—and even rude! Like my father! But I focused on the potential income. It would certainly alleviate some major financial burdens.

I soon found the "cottage," if one could call it that. It was an exact structural duplicate of the main mansion, only on a smaller scale. Its pinkish-beige stucco exterior made it a better fit in Vegas or Greece than out here in the heart of Napa.

Inside, the open-concept interior sported a large living area with two big beige sofas covered with throw pillows, a wine-colored La-Z-Boy lounger, another huge, golden recliner with its own ottoman, and a thick brown shag rug. On one wall was a huge stone fireplace with a mammoth plasma TV above it. Sliding glass doors just to the right of the fireplace opened out to a small, private stone patio with its own hot tub. Shrubs and lilac bushes surrounded the entire patio, filling the afternoon air with their glorious fragrance.

On the opposite side of the fireplace was a four-piece bath and a fully stocked galley kitchen with built-in appliances. A wooden door off the dining area led to the small, climate-controlled wine cellar, which housed some two hundred bottles. There'd be some good sipping going down if I chose to indulge.

Off to the other side of the galley kitchen, a staircase led up to a loft, which housed a king-size bed and a three-piece bathroom. Original art, some modern and some classic, adorned the walls.

Not too shabby, I thought, looking down at the living room from the upper level.

If I was going to spend the night, I figured I should make a few calls. First, I phoned Sadie to ask her to look in on my cat, Mouton.

Next, I dialed Julia.

"Where are you, hon?" she said as soon as she answered the phone. "I left a message on your machine and one on your cell."

I quickly checked, and I had in fact missed a call. Don't know how I didn't hear it!

"I'm in Napa on business," I said.

"Business? Monkey business, I'll bet. Are you behaving yourself?" she said, starting to laugh.

"Like a nun in a convent," I said.

"Right, and Elton John is dating Mariah Carey. So what's up, baby?" She seemed busy, and I could hear lots going on in her office while we chatted.

"Just wanted to let you know I'm spending the night here in Napa, at a client's house."

"And what's this client's name?" she said. "Is she gorgeous and can't keep her hands off you?"

I had to laugh.

"James McCall is a nice-looking man," I said, "but female and gorgeous he certainly is not. But who knows? If he wines me and dines me, maybe I'll let him get to second base."

Julia laughed. Then, she suddenly changed the subject: "Given any more thought to moving in together?"

Jarred by the abrupt switch of subjects, I hemmed and hawed.

She gave a huge sigh. "Just as I thought," she said.

There was an uncomfortable silence for a moment.

"Hold on for a moment, Woody," she said, as she addressed a work-related issue on her end. "Look, hon, I have to run," she said when she came back. "When are you coming home?"

"Tomorrow, late in the day," I said.

I had intended to ask a favor of her. I wanted her to sniff around her contacts at the Emporium to see if there was any suspicious activity involving a rare, old wine, but her sudden return to our moving-in dilemma put me off somewhat. So I decided not to. Besides, she was very busy.

"I'll call you in the morning," I said.

There was a moment's pause.

"Love you!" I said, throwing it out there.

"Me too." She hung up.

Finally, I dialed Charlie Cuddle, a great buddy of mine and a driver for a small courier company. I asked him to call all the agents on the International Beverage Network website who handle imported wine in California, pretending to be a rich socialite looking to buy some old, rare French vintages. He'd make notes of any agent who had anything.

Charlie and I grew up together in downtown San Francisco. In fact, Charlie spent so much time at my house, he knew more Jewish than many of my Jewish friends. Nowadays, in return for my mentoring him in the wine business he was eager to enter, he helped me with wine-related cases.

The International Beverage Network was a good place to start. Belonging to this association is voluntary, free, and definitely a good move for agents handling any kind of alcohol, including wine. The majority of members deal with retailers and many of the major chains as the liaison between supplier/distributor and seller. Many of them are award-winning agencies handling numerous major brands. Perhaps they had acquired the Chambertin somehow and were looking to sell it.

I pulled out my netbook, which I always have in my briefcase, and got online. I also pulled out my tape recorder to note any important finds. The first thing I wanted to do was look up Chambertin to further familiarize with it myself. I learned that, of the nine Grand Cru vineyards based around the French village of Gevrey-Chambertin, a mere two can legally use the name "Chambertin" without a caveat: the thirty-two-acre Le Chambertin and neighboring thirty-eight-acre Chambertin-Clos de Bèze vineyards.

Many of Burgundy's Grand Cru vineyards were owned by numerous entities on account of the breakdown of land back in the eighteenth century, but I wanted to see exactly how many owners of this Cru there were. As it turned out, there were twenty-three.

While surfing the net for info about Naopleon's 1784 Chambertin, I came across a very interesting note from a professor of vinous history from the University of Leeds in the UK. Although there had been no other mention, according to him, the wine was supposedly cursed. Throughout its history, it had been associated with much misfortune.

Cursed, eh? I chuckled.

When finished with my search, I grabbed my phone, my tape recorder, and a cold Heineken I found in the fridge. Losing my clothes, I went outside to settle in the hot tub for a while as I recorded some notes about the missing wine.

It's not that my memory stinks. It's great—just extremely short. Recording the details, no matter how trivial, not only helps me organize my thoughts, but often clarifies something I may have overlooked.

To my surprise, I felt unsettled. I couldn't shake the feeling I was being watched, but a rustle in the dense foliage beyond the hot tub turned out to be only a rabbit scampering through.

McCall's story seemed a bit convoluted to me, and a very small part of me wondered if he had staged the whole thing. McCall's refusal to let me search his room certainly didn't help his case. But, realistically speaking, too much evidence pointed to an actual theft. Somebody bypassed a very tight security system, entered the vault, took the wine, and got out, without anyone seeing them. All this would have been hard to accomplish without someone on the inside assisting.

Other than studying the crime scene, I hadn't yet done any real investigation, but my initial thought was that this whole theft megillah, if it really happened, sounded like security-system sabotage. The fact that the display unit showed the wine there when it wasn't could indicate "veiling," or "masking." This procedure, extremely common in heist movies, allowed an older visual to remain intact while the object or place itself was tampered with. But I needed to consult an expert for more details.

I got out of the tub, toweled down, put on a robe I found in a closet, and googled a couple security companies. I rang one in San Francisco, Jackson Security, pretending to be the proprietor of an upscale art gallery in Napa looking to install video equipment. Veiling, after all, wasn't just for theft. It was also used in art galleries and museums to display images of a piece of art or treasure not actually there because it was on loan, or because renovations or other work was underway. This way, the piece could still be seen by the public.

Occasionally, veiling was used to deceive folks. I knew a chap once who dealt in rare Chinese vases, and he would only display, through veiling, some of the items in his vault, even though there were many more in it. He didn't want buyers or prospective thieves to know exactly how much was there.

This is what I said I wanted to do when I spoke with Mr. Jackson himself, who was very familiar with the concept. He told me my idea of deception really defeats the purpose of a security system, especially if the system was a direct feed from camera to monitor—but, being a good businessman looking for a potential contract, he went along with me anyway. Though I knew veiling was controlled by computer, I wasn't sure of some of the details. I learned from Mr. Jackson that veiling could be controlled from any location, even from across the country, as long as the codes and control mechanisms were known. "Not all security systems are designed to accommodate this technique," he said. "It would have to be built in when created."

Next, and more importantly, I needed to talk with Touchstone Security. Inasmuch as they had installed the system, they would be the obvious culprits to sabotage it. In fact, maybe that's why they never looked inside the vault when they came to check it out.

On my way out, I stopped by the main house to get their address. When I asked McCall how he came to use that particular company, he told me that Johnny Spezzo, his friend Sam's son, had recommended them. The owner of the company, Joey Touchstone, was a security expert and an old Army buddy from back in Afghanistan.

I drove into the town of Napa looking for Touchstone Security. I found them downtown, housed in a small, one-story, detached structure with ground-to-ceiling glass windows and its own small parking lot.

Through the window, I could see the receptionist behind a desk and, on the walls, different cameras, alarms, and other security equipment. It was like a showroom. I tried the door, but it was locked. There was a buzzer, though, so I pushed it. The receptionist looked up from her work, gave me the once-over, and buzzed me in.

"Good day," I said. "I'm looking for a security system for my client's wine cellar in Sonoma, and a friend of mine, a client of yours, recommended you."

"Can I ask who the client is, sir?" the receptionist said, still looking me over.

"James McCall. He said to talk to the owner, Joey Touchstone."

"Just a moment, please," she said, heading into the back room. I could hear her speaking with someone.

In a few moments, she returned.

"Joey will be right with you," she said, taking her seat behind the desk.

I busied myself looking around the showroom at various closed-circuit cameras and monitors.

"Good afternoon, sir."

Turning around, I found an average-looking woman in what I guessed to be her early twenties, with brown hair and sharp features, wearing the kind of cat-eye glasses women wore in the fifties. She was dressed in a two-piece brown business suit.

"Good afternoon! I'm looking for the owner, Joey Touchstone," I said, looking past her for a man.

"That's me," she said. "Joanne Touchstone. Everyone calls me Joey."

Johnny Spezzo's old Army buddy was not at all what I expected.

"I understand Mr. McCall recommended us. He's a good customer," she said. "Unique system up there at his place! Had to custom-design it from scratch myself, Mr. . . .?"

"Robins," I said. "I'm looking for my system to have veiling capabilities, just like Mr. McCall's."

"His system isn't set up for veiling," she said. "There's no reason for it."

That's interesting, I thought.

I passed her a card. As she looked down at it and saw my wine credentials, she tilted her head and looked at me strangely, as if trying to figure something out.

"This wouldn't by any chance have something to do with the theft of Mr. McCall's wine?" she said.

Shrewd woman—she somehow managed to put two and two together. But I played dumb.

"Whatever do you mean?"

"Come on, Mr. Robins! That line about wanting a security system with veiling for a wine collection? That's bogus. What would be the point? And 'like Mr. McCall's'? You didn't expect me to fall for that crap, did you?"

Realizing she was quite the smart cookie, I reluctantly admitted that she was right.

"Look, I don't have to talk to you," she said, changing her tone of voice and starting to walk away.

"Would you prefer to talk to the police?" I said, pulling out my phone.

"All right, all right!" she said, turning. "I checked out his system and it was fine. Whatever happened there was not the fault of the system."

"You yourself checked it out?" I said, pointing at her.

"Me and only me. If I design a system, I'm the one who maintains it."

"You're sure there was nothing wrong with it?"

"Look, mister, I know my business," she said. "I went over it thoroughly and found nothing wrong."

"And why didn't you check inside the vault?"

"No point! All security control mechanisms are on the outside," she said. "Unless someone bore through the two and a half feet of solid steel, they must have entered by punching in the code and opening the door."

"And how do you explain the image of the wine on the screen on a system not set up for veiling?"

"I—I can't," she said. "I don't know how that could have happened."

I wasn't sure I believed her about the veiling and still thought she was involved somehow in the theft. As I left, I grabbed a card from Touchstone, then drove back to the estate.

CHAPTER 6

O nce back at the cottage, I added a few more notes to my tape recorder. It was still late afternoon, with plenty of time until dinner, so I decided to drive around to the main house and start looking into things. The kitchen off the living room belonged in a hotel, not a home. There was top-of-the-line stainless-steel equipment everywhere. Wolfgang Puck, eat your heart out!

But though the kitchen was large, it wasn't so big that I couldn't find a cup of coffee. As I started searching, I heard cursing from a doorway just outside the corner. Stepping closer to the open door, I could tell it wasn't the English language tainting the afternoon air. I peered outside and saw a rather stout fellow in his mid-thirties with curly, dark hair and a thick moustache, kneeling over what appeared to be herbs of some sort. He was dressed in chef whites, complete with fluffy hat.

"If I catch you, I'll kill you," he mumbled as he pulled greens right out of the ground. On a closed-in wooden deck like an oversized window box, there was a little garden oasis, overloaded with all kinds of herbs, like oregano, basil, thyme, and marjoram.

When the chef heard me approaching, he stood up quickly, somewhat startled.

"Excuse, me, *signore!*" he said. "Some damn animal has been eating my basil."

Although I could appreciate his dilemma—I have an herb and veggie garden myself and know the woes of keeping wildlife at bay—I couldn't keep from snickering. With his white chef's hat and dark moustache, the guy looked like he had just jumped off the label of some canned pasta brand.

"I'm Woody Robins," I said, introducing myself.

"Yes, Mr. McCall said you would be around asking questions. Roberto Rossi at your service."

I asked if he knew why I would be asking questions. He said he didn't, and when I told him, he was shocked.

"Who would steal from Mr. McCall?" he said.

"That's what I'm here to find out. Where were you the night the wine went missing?" I said, leaning against the doorway.

"Here in the kitchen, cooking the whole time," he said, wiping his hands on what appeared to be a dishtowel.

"Do you use wine in your cooking, Roberto? May I call you Roberto?"

"Of course."

"Well, do you?" I said, cocking my head to one side.

"Often," he said.

I then asked if he used French wine, then Burgundy, and, finally, Grand Cru red Burgundy. He answered yes to the first two, but didn't seem to know what Grand Cru was.

"You know—expensive French red wine? Maybe in a large bottle?"

"No, *signore*, only small bottles."

I wondered if he was lying about not knowing what a Grand Cru Burgundy was. Every chef I knew had a great working knowledge of wine. They were taught about it at chef school and, like Roberto, often used it in their dishes.

"When you use wine in your cooking, Roberto, do you go down to the wine cellar and get it yourself?" I said.

He said he didn't have to. Swinging open a cupboard next to the pantry, he revealed about fifteen bottles, mostly Italian and Californian reds and whites, with a few lower-end French.

"What happens when you need more?" I said, examining the labels.

"Ms. Svenson or Mr. Lambeck get it for me."

"Who's this Mr. Lambeck?"

"Mr. McCall's butler," he said. I recalled McCall mentioning a "man-servant."

"And you never go down to the cellar to get it yourself?"

"No! I'm not even sure where the *vino* is kept," he said. "Besides, I don't have a key."

"If you're not sure where the wine is kept, how do you know it requires a key?" I said, looking at him strangely.

"I'm only guessing," he said, shifting from foot to foot.

I asked if he'd needed Svenson or Lambeck to retrieve any wine the night of the theft, but Roberto said he had plenty already.

"Who else came into the kitchen that night while you were cooking?" I said.

"Only Ms. Svenson and Mr. Lambeck—they were serving the food."

As I looked around the room, discovering no bottle, Roberto told me a bit about his background. He was born and raised in Tuscany, but studied in Veneto, and actually worked in Piedmont for a couple years. He had even done a stint at a five-star bistro in Paris (which was all the more reason he should know what a Grand Cru Burgundy was). "My cooking is a complex blend of many regions and cultures," he said. "I love to experiment."

"All right, Roberto," I said. "That'll do for now. Can I have a look in your room?"

Agreeing, Roberto led me upstairs to the second floor and down to the end of the hallway. Taking a quick look around his medium-sized room, nicely decorated in beige and ivory with a queen bed, dresser, large easy chair, and substantial closet, I found no wine.

"So where can a guy get a cup of coffee around here?" I said as we left his room and returned downstairs to the kitchen.

"Sit down. I'll make you one. Would you like a cappuccino?"

"Please!"

While Roberto prepared my *café*, I stepped outside onto the patio to take in the view It faced north, and as far as the eye could see, there were rolling hills, greenery, and, of course, grapevines. While out there, my mind shifted back to Julia and our dilemma—or, should I say, my fear. I hoped she would be patient while I worked out my issues. She was so sweet, and I really did love her, but I was gun-shy. I so didn't want our relationship to fail like most of those I saw growing up! I wanted to avoid not only a broken heart but, if we lived together, all the hassle and aggravation of dividing stuff up and moving out.

Roberto emerged from the kitchen with a tray holding my cappuccino and some homemade biscotti. It tasted divine. When finished, I took the tray back into the kitchen.

"Grazie mille," I said to Roberto.

"Ah, you speak Italian?"

"Not really," I said, shaking my head.

From there, I ventured further into the house in search of Mr. Lambeck—McCall's manservant, as he called him. I hadn't thought anybody in this day and age called a butler a "manservant." It seemed so archaic.

I found Lambeck upstairs in the "master's" boudoir. It was humongous, containing a gigantic, ornate bed, numerous couches, easy chairs, several bureaus and dressers, a baby grand piano, and two balconies. The entire space was decorated in muted shades, with fine art on the walls. Lambeck was straightening up McCall's closet, if you could call it that. The closet was an entire twenty-by-twenty-foot room off the bedroom, with wall-to-wall hangers, shelves, and shoe racks filled to the brim with clothes and footwear. It even had an automatic shoe polisher, the kind one finds in the loo of stuffy, private men's clubs.

I called out Lambeck's name, but he was too engrossed in his tidying. So I stepped up and knocked on the closet door. This time, he heard me.

"Ah, you must be Mr. Robins. You wish to see me?" he said, speaking in what sounded like some sort of British accent.

"Yes, Mr. Lambeck. May I have a few minutes of your time?"

"Certainly, sir."

I explained why I was there. He too seemed extremely surprised to learn about the theft. "I thought you were a business associate of Mr. McCall's," he said.

I asked him about his background, and learned that Michael Lambeck had come to America from England, where he had been a butler, when he heard there was lots of money to be made here in the trade. Of his total three and a half years in America, the last two had been spent in California, and just over a year with McCall. Previously, he had worked at an upscale, private men's club in New York called the Empire Club.

As he spoke, I noticed he had an interesting habit of raising his left eyebrow—at least, I assumed it was his left eyebrow. Really, he only had a single thick unibrow running across his entire forehead, like a pasted-on cat's tail.

He appeared to be from the old school—prim, proper, and all that rot. Completely formal, he was impeccably attired in a crisp linen shirt, houndstooth tie, waistcoat, and dark flannel slacks, even though it was probably eighty degrees outside. He had to be in his late fifties. He was a tall man, slender, with closely cropped, touched-up brown hair, brown eyes, and a perfect complexion, obviously spa-treated. He gave off a faint aroma of aftershave.

"What part of England do you hail from, Mr. Lambeck?"

"From London's West End, sir," he said. "I grew up there."

"That's funny," I said. "You don't sound like a West End Londoner—or a Londoner at all."

Though I had spent a fair bit of time in London studying wine early in my life, I couldn't really tell if his accent was authentic or not. I was just testing him, but I could tell the question made him uncomfortable.

"I suppose my accent has been homogenized somewhat from living in different places."

"Tell me, Mr. Lambeck," I said, "what do you know of Mr. McCall's wine collection?"

"I know Mr. McCall has a magnificent cellar with hundreds of bottles of fine wine, but I certainly wasn't aware that one was missing. Besides, Ms. Svenson always deals with the wine."

That's funny, I thought. *The chef said Svenson and Lambeck both retrieved wine for him.*

"Do you like wine, Mr. Lambeck?"

"No, I'm a gin and tonic man, sir."

"Ms. Svenson tells me you spend a fair bit of time on the lower level of the house," I lied. "Doing what?"

"That's not true," Lambeck said, getting defensive. "The only time I'm down there is to clean and retrieve something, sir." He started to sweat.

When asked if he ever went into the game room, he informed me that he had to clean in there, too. I asked about his access to the wine cellar. Again, he said it was Svenson's domain, and she was the only one with the key.

"If you don't go into the wine cellar, how do you know it requires a key to open it?" I said.

"I only assume, sir." He was again getting fidgety.

I asked him about the night the wine went missing, but he hadn't noticed anything suspicious that day.

"Wait a moment," he said, remembering that night. "In fact, I thought I heard some footsteps on the stairs leading to the lower level, but when I went to investigate, I found no one."

"Approximately what time did you hear these footsteps?"

"About 9 p.m.," he said after thinking about it.

"And no one from the dinner table was missing?"

"I really didn't notice, sir."

He was "sir"-ing me so much, I felt like I had been knighted by the queen.

We left McCall's room, and I briefly searched Lambeck's. It was huge and nicely appointed. There was a four-poster king-size bed, a large couch, several lounge chairs, an oak bureau, a huge closet, a three-piece bathroom, and a desk with a computer and printer. The room even had its own small balcony. Ornate framed paintings and a gilded mirror decorated the walls. No wine bottle was found.

As soon as we finished talking, Lambeck immediately went back to work, systematically organizing the boss's wardrobe. *Boy, he's a barrel of laughs,* I thought. Whether his accent was authentic or not, I couldn't tell, but it *did* sound odd.

I ran into Ms. Svenson in the hall and asked if she had a few moments to answer some questions, but she was "extremely busy with unexpected chores that needed tending to immediately," or something like that. I was a little suspicious—something in her voice, I suppose—but I agreed.

With no one else about to talk to, I went outside and took a walk around some of the property to check out access to the house. From what I could see, the estate was entirely surrounded by a monitored fence, with the only entrance at the main gate. The estate was indeed gorgeous, a world unto itself.

At about half past five, I drove back to the cottage and took a shower. The main bathroom had one of those multi-nozzle jobbies that sprays you at different levels and angles. I felt like a car going through an automatic carwash.

Sometime later, I got dressed to the sounds of Sinatra and Tommy Dorsey's big band, recorded in 1940. Ol' Blue Eyes at his finest! Man, few can hold a candle to Frankie. It's clear why—his phrasing, timbre, and easy delivery are legendary. One of my greatest regrets is that I never saw him perform live.

As Dorsey swung and Sinatra delivered, I prepared for the evening. Donned in the same clothes I had arrived in—a pair of cream-colored, pleated cotton slacks, a Hawaiian shirt of burnt sienna and gold, and a pair of buttery leather Gucci loafers, sans socks, all beneath a straw fedora and a golden brown bandana—I was good to go.

CHAPTER 7

I t was such a warm, lovely evening, I left my wheels behind and walked up to the house. I meandered through trees and gardens, over a babbling brook via a small stone bridge, and past a well-lit tennis court spilling out onto an open area at the back of the main house. A large, beautiful, kidney-shaped pool, surrounded by a huge interlocking brick patio adorned with umpteen garden umbrellas, tables, and loungers, dominated the scene. It looked like something out of *The Great Gatsby*. I felt right at home.

Soft music and laughter emerged from the upper patio that ran directly off the back of the house, the same one on which I had earlier enjoyed my cappuccino and biscotti. I made my way up the stairs to check out the frivolity.

As I neared the top, a tennis ball came bouncing by. I caught it.

"Tennis, anyone?" I said, tossing the ball up and down.

There were three gals—the twins and an older woman—and two guys at the bar at the top, alongside several cushioned wicker chairs, a small sofa, side tables, and a larger round table set for dinner.

The older woman and one of the twins were laughing hysterically, eyes on the tennis ball.

"I'm so sorry," said the older woman, who I assumed was McCall's sister, as she calmed down. "Emmy here was demonstrating how she accidentally beaned her tennis partner in the ya-yas today, and the ball got away from her. Then when you came up the stairs looking like *Miami Vice* in Honolulu—"

"I'll take that as a compliment, my dear," I said, putting the ball down on the bar.

"I'm Patricia, James's sister," she said. "This is my husband, Horace.

And you must be Mr. Robins."

"If I must be, then I won't deny it."

There was no mistaking who Patricia was. She had her brother's bone structure and piercing blue peepers. I made her out to be in her late fifties with auburn hair. When we shook hands, her grip was extremely firm. You can tell a lot about a person from their handshake.

Her husband, on the other hand, seemed disinterested. He went through the motions of courtesy, but acted as if he wanted to be somewhere else. A stout, large, balding man about Patricia's age, he had a bit of a paunch, bushy, brown eyebrows, and a rosy complexion that probably came from drinking too much. Call it first impressions or whatever, but I took an immediate dislike to him.

"And these are my nieces, Emily and Denise," said Patricia. "Denise is single and available."

"Oh, Aunt Patricia!" Denise said, starting to blush.

Aside from their dress, the women were like two identical and stunning bookends. Emily offered her hand for shaking, and I obliged.

"I'm Woody Robins," I said, disengaging Emily's hand.

"The pleasure is all mine, Mr. Robins," she said, gazing into my eyes.

I can most emphatically assure you, dear reader, the pleasure wasn't all hers.

"Please," I said, "call me Woody."

I would have greeted Denise the same way, but she didn't offer her hand. All she said was, "Hey."

The ladies were in their early twenties, and up close, I discovered I'd actually underestimated their beauty. Silky, baby-fine blonde hair fell about mid-back. Full, pouty, luscious lips sat below those McCall blue eyes, which were riveting on them.

Emily wore a short red skirt with an ivory-colored short-sleeved cotton blouse, unbuttoned enough to reveal a lacy, silk camisole beneath. Her magnificently unadorned and tapered gams flowed down into a pair of sexy red sling-backs.

Denise, on the other hand, was still in her blue jeans and cowboy shirt, and I detected the faint smell of saddle leather and hay.

To say I was taken with their beauty would be like calling steak tartare hamburger.

The tall, good-looking, clean-shaven chap about their age at the bar smiled away at me and cleared his throat.

"Oh, and this is my boyfriend, Johnny Spezzo," Emily said.

So this is Johnny Spezzo, I thought. He came forward and shook my hand.

"A pleasure to meet you," he said, a big smile on his face.

I recalled that not only had Johnny Spezzo recommended Touch-stone, but McCall had mentioned that he and his parents had been present the night the wine went missing.

Emily insisted I sit next to her on the couch. I couldn't understand why, when her boyfriend was there, but it didn't seem to fizz on him. Maybe she was just being sociable.

I noticed a bottle of Roederer Estate Anderson Valley Brut bubbly uncorked in an ice bucket on the bar. Patricia poured me a flute.

Just then, McCall emerged from the house onto the patio, asking for Johnny's help on his computer. Apparently, he was a computer whiz kid. I excused myself and followed them in. My hope was perhaps to catch some sort of dialogue between the two about the missing wine. If questioned, I would simply say that I, too, often had computer problems, and maybe I could pick up a hint or two on how to solve them.

McCall's screen was frozen, and the computer was making a weird hissing sound. Johnny sat down at the computer and started punching in all kinds of codes.

"This can happen when too many programs are open at the same time," he said. "However, it could be a virus. There's a real nasty one out there that'll freeze your screen with whatever is on it at the time. You'll need major help to repair it."

Fortunately for McCall, it wasn't a virus, and within two minutes, the computer was working properly again. I was impressed. Johnny and I returned to the patio while McCall finished what he was doing. A few minutes later, he emerged.

"I'm glad you've all gotten acquainted," he said. He grabbed the bottle of Roederer from the ice bucket on the bar, poured himself a glass, and topped everyone off.

"Do you need a refill, Horace?" he said. Horace appeared to be slugging a whiskey of sorts.

"Dandy," said Horace. "It's the Lagavulin." He gave McCall his glass.

McCall went over to the bar, dropped a couple of ice cubes into Horace's glass, and poured a good four fingers of the Islay single malt Scotch. *Horace may be miserable*, I thought, *but he has good taste in whiskey*.

McCall's presence, with his stern demeanor and abrupt, commanding attitude, changed the mood somewhat, but the group still chatted amiably about the heat, airport security, baseball (of which I'm a huge fan, especially the Giants), wine, and even the price of pork bellies. It gave me a chance to get to know these folks, particularly McCall and the ladies.

From what I could gather, theirs was old money, originating from horse-breeding in the mid-east generations ago. McCall's grandfather, an avid wine lover, moved west in the 1950s, settled in Napa, and started buying up vineyard property in the Russian River Valley of Sonoma nearer the Pacific Ocean and here in Carneros in southern Napa—all long before California was ever considered a decent place to grow the finicky Pinot Noir grape. He must have had the gift of clairvoyance, because today, both regions are probably the best growing areas in the state for Pinot Noir. His son and grandson, astute businessmen themselves, embraced that love of wine and vineyards, and today, the family owned more acreage of prime Pinot grape-growing real estate than anyone in the state.

Throughout the conversation, Emily and Denise bickered frequently about nothing important that I could see. Movies, clothes, music! They just plain didn't seem to like each other, and each jumped all over what the other said. McCall had to step in several times to calm them down.

Horace, meanwhile, was basically incommunicado. When he did say something, it was a grumpy criticism, and he got up several times to top off his glass—not that I was counting, mind you. I wondered if he was trying to drown some sort of sorrow.

Johnny Spezzo took an active part in the conversation, telling the occasional anecdote about his armed forces days. He was quite charming, and I could see why Emily liked him.

In the middle of a story Emily was telling about her time at New York University, Ms. Svenson announced that dinner was ready. We shifted to the dinner table.

"Woody, you sit here next to me," Emily said, tapping the chair she wanted me in.

"Yes, ma'am," I said, looking in Johnny's direction to see his reaction. There was none. He just smiled.

By this time, my stomach was doing backflips. I hadn't had a bite to eat since that biscotti, and the crisp acidity of the Roederer had my gastronomic juices flowing. Before the food arrived, though, McCall got up, went behind the bar and, from another ice bucket, retrieved a chilled bottle of 2006 St. Supéry Sauvignon Blanc from California. He poured a slosh into the empty glass in front of me.

"Robins, would you be so kind as to check this and make sure it's okay?" he said.

Oh, it's "Robins" now, is it? I thought. I picked up the glass, sniffed it, and took a hit. The nose was vibrant, with gooseberry, melon, and citrus, while the palate was crisp, fresh, and lively. "Squeaky clean," I said, taking another sniff.

Upon my approval, McCall set about pouring glasses for everyone, including Horace.

"How did you get that?" Emily said, leaning over and looking toward the scar on my left hand, above the thumb.

"I cut it open trying to use a saber to take off the top of a bottle of bubbly in France a number of years back," I said, rubbing the spot.

The trolley Ms. Svenson guided onto the patio contained the first course. The aroma was so fabulous my nostrils actually flared in anticipation, like a horse before the first race. My small plate was provided with a lone langoustine, drizzled with a dressing of some sort and herbs. The smell of garlic wafted up from it. One bite and I was in heaven. With the wine, the dish was nirvana. I used some crusty bread to mop up the residue. (I'm a peasant. So sue me.)

Distracted though I was by the food, I couldn't help but notice Ms. Svenson staring occasionally at McCall with an interesting blend of disdain and longing. It was odd.

I don't know how the conversation turned to school, but Emily and McCall wound up in a heated argument about tuition fees.

"You should work for your tuition," McCall said. "That's the only way you'll appreciate the value of education."

"Why should I? We have money. You don't think twice about supporting the stable, horses, and all of *her* riding lessons," Emily said, nodding in Denise's direction.

"I work for that! I brush the horses and clean out the stables," Denise said, quite ticked off. "Besides, I don't get half of what I need for competitions."

"You were always the favorite. It's just not fair."

"Now, stop it, the both of you!" said Patricia, standing. "Need I remind you that we have company?"

Ms. Svenson reappeared to clear the dishes. When she finished, she left, then soon returned with a carafe of red wine, from which she poured a glass for everyone. I wondered why McCall hadn't asked me to try this one.

"This is a 1990 Martha's Vineyard Cabernet to accompany the Steak

Florentine. Ms. Svenson has already checked it for stability," he said, as if reading my mind. Noticing my somewhat puzzled look, he added, "She's a certified sommelier."

"So Ms. Svenson is not only a very efficient housekeeper, but a wine expert to boot," I said. "How unusual and wonderful."

"More like my house manager," said McCall. "She literally runs this place. I found her working as a sommelier in an upscale restaurant in St. Helena some twenty-six years ago. She can do a little plumbing, and electrical and mechanical stuff, better than most men! She's been with me ever since, save the one year she went back home."

"You're a very lucky man, sir," I said, lifting my glass and tipping it to Ms. Svenson.

Then I took a sniff. The irresistible black fruit, truffles, coffee, tobacco, and chocolate enveloped my senses. A sip brought to life sublime ripe tannins, a supple mouth feel, and great length. How delicious! *If nothing else pans out, at least the wine is good*, I thought.

I was somewhat surprised, though, that McCall wasn't serving any Pinot Noir. You'd think he'd want to showcase wine made from his own fruit.

Later in the evening, after some homemade gelato and an espresso, Johnny announced that he had to leave. He shook my hand again and said how nice it was to meet me. Emily showed him out, and I could hear them chatting and laughing in the distance. Patricia and her now somewhat drunken husband headed inside—evidently, they were spending the night.

On her return, Emily asked if I would like to go for a stroll through the garden. I was surprised and wondered what Johnny would make of it if he were still present.

But just as we got up to depart, McCall took me aside and asked if I found my digs comfortable—and if I would be starting my investigation the next day. I told him that I was extremely comfortable at the cottage, that I had already started my investigation with some of the staff, and that I would continue the next morning.

I bid him goodnight, thanking him for the meal as Emily and I headed out to the garden.

CHAPTER 8

B y now, the sun had set, and a big boss moon and a million twinkling stars filled the night sky. A light breeze gently caressed our brows as we strolled.

"This was a really good idea," I said to Emily, breaking the silence. "I'm so full. Do you folks eat like that all the time?"

"When there's company!" she said. "Father likes to entertain. It's his excuse to uncork a bottle or two. In case you hadn't noticed, he loves his wine. It's one of the only things he doesn't mind spending money on."

"What did you study at NYU?" I said, making conversation.

"Sociology," she said. "In fact, I have a master's."

"Beauty and brains," I said. "Do you mind if I ask why you went to school back east?"

"Had to get away from my father," she said, immediately sounding angry. "He's such a damn control freak."

I just stared at her. As soon as she said it, her expression changed and her face contorted. I wondered if I had opened a can of worms.

"Wants to manipulate everything and everyone around him!"

I tried to change the subject by asking what aspect of sociology was her focus, but she ignored me and continued complaining about her father.

"Can you believe I had to take money out of my trust fund to pay for college?" said Emily. "He wouldn't cough it up unless I stayed here. He just wanted me under his thumb so he could control my life."

I could certainly relate to that. I remembered my own father.

"I'm glad I went, though," she said. "I had my freedom. And then he has the gall to give me that line about earning money for something you want in order to appreciate its value. The man infuriates me."

I gazed down at the ground as she ranted on. Obviously, the girl needed to vent. I was surprised, though, that she would do so with basically a complete stranger. It made me feel very uncomfortable.

When Emily saw my reaction, she realized what she was doing. There was a moment of silence before she spoke again.

"Sorry about that, Woody," she said, regaining her composure. "Didn't mean to dump this on you!"

I nodded, but the girl obviously had some serious issues with her father. As we strolled along a little further, she continued to tell me why she chose New York.

"It's so vibrant and alive," she said. "It has the best and the worst of everything. People are real there. The circles my family flows in are lots of fluffs and cardboard cutouts."

"And why sociology?" I said, quite curious.

Emily told me she really liked people. Born into wealth, and knowing how privileged she was, she had always wanted to help the less fortunate, ever since she was a little girl. As part of her practicum while working on her master's, she was assigned to a drop-in center for abused kids in Queens and loved it. Since she had come back home, she put in a day every week at a drop-in center in downtown Napa.

I looked into her eyes as she spoke about this, and she appeared to be sincere.

"So why did you come back?" I said.

"My mother! I came home to help out when she got sick. It was a terrible time." She started to tear up. "If it weren't for my father . . ." She stopped herself.

I wondered what she was going to say, but decided not to pursue it at the moment. I didn't want to start her ranting again. But I could also see talking about her mother was making her sad, so I changed the subject.

"Johnny seems like a nice guy."

"Johnny's a sweetheart, and extremely charming."

I had thought the same thing.

"I love him dearly. He really likes kids. He'll make a great father."

I could only assume from that remark that wedding plans and a family were in their future.

"I know he really loves me. He treats me well. He's extremely kind. I only wish he were more passionate—that he'd show more public displays of affection," she said. "Never seems to get jealous when I talk to other guys, either!"

He *was* rather complacent over dinner, especially when Emily insisted I sit next to her. In his place, I certainly would have had some stirrings of jealousy. *Wait a minute*, I thought. *Is she implying that she's interested in me, or was she just trying to get a reaction from Johnny?* If it was the latter, I really didn't like being used that way.

"I understand Johnny was in the armed forces," I said.

"That's right."

"What did he do over there?" I said.

"He was a computer/surveillance expert."

That's probably how he and Touchstone met. It didn't take a rocket scientist to figure that, together, they were prime suspects and could surely figure out how to dismantle the security in such a way that it would look like the system was not at fault. But that still didn't explain exactly how they lifted the double magnum undetected. There had to have been an inside connection.

I wanted to ask about her rocky relationship with her sister, but I dared not, judging from her rant about her father—and that question hadn't even been direct.

"I assume your father told you about his stolen wine," I said.

"That's all he's been going on about since it happened."

"Is there anything at all you can tell me about the night the wine went missing?" I said, not wanting to press any further on personal issues. "Anything unusual about the evening?"

"Not that I can think of," she said, thinking about it.

"How about people? Anybody act suspicious?"

"No." She hesitated a bit, then started to say something, but again stopped.

"What? Is there something you want to tell me?" I said.

"It's not important," she said, "and it really has nothing to do with the dinner party."

"Why don't you let me decide whether it's important? What is it?"

She proceeded to tell me about the chauffeur, Dan Amos.

"He makes me uncomfortable," she said. "Maybe I'm judging him by appearances, but he always looks like a little boy with his hand in the cookie jar."

Emily told me that she had made her concerns known to her father, but of course, he said it was just her imagination. Still, Amos wasn't at the dinner that night, and usually wasn't even in the house.

"What about Horace?" I said.

"Uncle Horace?"

"He doesn't seem like a particularly happy sort," I said, treading carefully.

"He's okay—just not a very good businessman, I suppose."

I wondered what she meant by that, but didn't feel it was the right time to ask. I'd find out somehow, though.

We stopped on the stone bridge over the stream.

"Look, Woody, down in the water. A bullfrog!" said Emily, pointing down toward the bank.

Sure enough, next to some footprints in the mud that looked like they were made by a heeled shoe, a big old bullfrog sat on a rock on the bank, puffing itself up, like frogs do. Suddenly, its tongue shot out, and it nabbed a fly. Emily was like a little child who had just discovered Easter eggs. She clapped her hands with delight and grinned. Standing on the bridge in the moonlight, she looked positively enchanting.

Then, suddenly, Emily spurted out, "Can I come back to the cottage for a nightcap?"

I was taken aback by the request and, feeling a little uncomfortable, didn't know what to say. She had just told me how much she loved her boyfriend. I wondered what her intentions were. She couldn't still have been trying to get a jealous reaction out of Johnny. He wasn't even here. Maybe she was still just being sociable—or maybe, just maybe, she really was interested in me. I didn't know, and I was confused. If she *was* interested, I certainly didn't need this complication. I was having enough problems committing to living with Julia.

So I declined. Emily looked hurt and gave me a pout that just about changed my mind.

Back at the cottage, I recorded some observations about dinner and bits of info I had learned. Who knew if they would come in handy later? But as I fell asleep, I found myself pondering why Emily had wanted to come back to the cottage with me.

CHAPTER 9

U p at the house the next morning a bit before 11 a.m., I ran into Ms. Svenson and asked if she could afford a couple minutes to chat. Once again she put me off, but she did give me the Yountville address of Manuel Rodrigo, the gardener—he was off work today—so I went there instead.

In twelve minutes or so, I was in the heart of Yountville. Manuel Rodrigo lived right on Highway 29, above a restaurant called the Country Kitchen. I found the place easily enough and parked out front. I could see what looked like a flat or apartment above the restaurant, but could find no entrance. I walked around the building twice, to no avail. But the windows above were open, so I started calling out his name. Nothing!

Finally, the front door of the restaurant opened, and a guy in an apron came out.

"What's all the ruckus? I'm running a business here," he said, wiping his hands on his apron.

"I'm looking for the guy who lives upstairs."

"Oh, he's inside having a coffee."

I followed him in, and the guy pointed out Rodrigo, a small man in his late twenties, maybe early thirties, with jet-black hair, an olive complexion, and brown eyes. Dressed in light cotton beige work pants, a blousy off-white shirt with a red bandana tied loosely around his neck, and a pair of dirty sneakers, he looked like he was ready for work, not a day off. I went over to him and introduced myself, told him why I was there, and asked if I could take a look around his place upstairs. He quickly finished his coffee and led me through the kitchen to a stairway just inside the back door. (No wonder I couldn't find it.)

I followed him up to a dark, one-bedroom apartment, sparsely decorated with secondhand, mismatched furnishings: a melamine dining table and chairs from the 1950s; a scuffed-up, tattered easy chair; and veneered end tables. The shabby couch in the small living room was made up like a bed.

"Does anyone else live here with you?" I said, looking around.

"Just my cousin. He's up helping out with the vintage."

He offered me a seat, and I accepted. "Where are you from?" I said.

"Tijuana." Rodrigo, like so many of his countrymen, came up to work the harvest from April or so to October. He'd been doing it about three years now.

"So how'd you get into the gardening side of things?" I said, crossing my legs.

He explained that he had shown a particular knack for tending the other crops and growth around the vineyards, so McCall took him on as his full-time gardener. Because he had no immediate family back home, save perhaps his cousin, it was a good move.

"I'm working to save enough money to go to school for viticulture," he said.

We talked a little bit about grape-growing, of which he actually knew a fair bit already. He was polite and well-spoken, and would probably make a decent viticulturist, once trained.

"Do you ever go into the house at the estate, Mr. Rodrigo?"

"I have no reason to. Besides, I'm not allowed," he said.

When questioned about his whereabouts the night of May 30, he simply said he was at home with his cousin. I asked where his cousin was at that moment, and he informed me he was working.

He went into the kitchen and pulled a soda out of the fridge. He offered me one, but I declined. He sat down in a chair next to me. He seemed to be a little nervous as he tapped his fingers on one of the end tables. It made me wonder if his immigration papers were in order.

"Do you know what red Burgundy is, Mr. Rodrigo?" I said.

"No."

"Do you mind if I have a look around?"

"Be my guest."

I took a quick look through the rest of the living room and kitchen, but there was nothing of any value or significance—only some books on gardening and viticulture, a toaster oven, and dirty dishes in the sink. The same applied to the bedroom, except for one thing: Among a pile of photos of Mexico was a folded-up poster explaining how to read a French wine label. I thought that very odd, because he had said he didn't know what red Burgundy was.

When I came back out of the bedroom with the poster in hand, I asked him about it.

He started to sweat.

"I picked it up at a wine shop here in town so I could learn about French wine, but I have not gotten around to looking at it," he said.

"And you simply forgot you had it?"

"Yes," he said. He was starting to get real nervous now.

"I would think that Mr. McCall, being a Pinot grower and Pinot being the same grape that's in red Burgundy, might have made a reference to it at some point."

"I don't remember," was all he said as he looked away.

I thanked him for his time and showed myself out.

I didn't know what to make of the poster or what he said. Was the guy lying to me?

CHAPTER 10

I thought it might be a good idea to track down Patricia and Horace Botner next. I called Ms. Svenson to see if they were still at the house, but she told me they had left for home bright and early. They lived in the train-stop town of Oakville, a short drive north of Yountville.

Their house was a sprawling, ranch-style bungalow with a double garage on what looked like a well-manicured acre or so of land. Patricia herself answered the door. I wondered where the housekeeper was. With the money her family had, you would expect one, but maybe it was her day off. Patricia informed me that the hubby was out back by the pool.

The house was nothing like her brother's. Modern, chic furnishings with fine lines and abstract art lined the walls. The entire space was open-concept, with high ceilings, skylights, and both track and recessed lighting. It was extremely elegant and, frankly, far removed from what I would have expected.

Once we got to the back patio doors, I spotted a blob, which I assumed was Horace, floating on an air mattress in the deep end of the pool, a drink in hand.

Before long, I was lying in one of the loungers next to Patricia, who was completely covered in a light, long-sleeved floral jumpsuit of sorts, with a big-rimmed straw hat and sunglasses. She offered me a sandwich and a cocktail Ms. Svenson had created called a Skinny Dane—equal parts aquavit, brandy, and gin with a splash of orange juice, all over lots of crushed ice with a lime wedge.

"Be mindful of that," Patricia said. "It packs quite a punch."

"Not to worry, my dear," I said. "I was a boy scout. Always prepared!" But one sip and I knew what she meant. It was delicious and refreshing, but, wow, was it potent! By the looks of the beached whale on the air mattress in the water at the other end of the pool, I guessed Horace was on number three or four. Patricia yelled to the floating lump in the deep end to come have some food. Nearly catatonic, he ignored her.

"I don't know what to do with him," Patricia said, looking very concerned. "He's been so depressed lately. He's drinking like a fish." She shook her head.

"If you don't mind my asking, Patricia, why is he like that?"

Horace was far enough away that he couldn't hear our conversation, and quite out of it besides.

"Oh, he's a pain in the ass these days," she said. "Lost his dry-cleaning business because of a stupid investment. He's tried several other things, but all have failed. He's basically broke. And when I found out he was playing poker with money he didn't have, with Lambeck and some of his buddies, I hit the roof."

Patricia stopped herself, perhaps realizing she was saying too much to basically a stranger. But I wondered how Horace could be broke. Patricia obviously came from a very well-to-do family. Even if Horace had lost his business, you would think she at least had some money of her own. More to the point, I wondered what Horace was doing hanging with Lambeck.

Just then, we heard a loud splash. I turned to find that Horace had tipped over into the pool. He was submerged, and he wasn't moving.

Patricia screamed.

Quickly, I jumped up, knocking my drink into the pool, and dove into the water. Rising to take a deep breath, I swam under, grabbed Horace, and, straining, pulled him to the surface and towed him to the side of the pool.

He was unconscious, so I immediately started mouth-to-mouth, to the best of my ability, right there in the water. I had never done it before, but had seen it enough in the movies and on TV. I wasn't even sure if I was doing it right. He was so soused it was like sucking on a still. It must have done some good, though, because after about thirty seconds, Horace came to, coughing and spitting up water.

"Are you okay, Horace?" I said, still holding onto him.

"Stop kissing me," he said.

"You're welcome," I replied, giving him a dirty look.

I climbed out of the water, then helped Patricia pull Horace out. Crying, Patricia held her husband.

"You stupid, stupid man," she said, cuddling him and stroking his forehead.

There was the crux of the matter. Even though he was a poor businessman, had become a drunk, and was obviously making this woman's life miserable, she still loved him. Love is blind, dontcha know.

"I suggest you stay out of the pool the rest of the day, Horace," I said.

Patricia led him over to a lounger, where he lay down. She grabbed a beach towel and covered him, then ran over in my direction and threw one around me.

"Are you okay?" she said, still sniffling.

"I'm fine," I said, my heart still racing and my adrenalin pumping. "I could really use another one of those Skinny Danes, if you don't mind. I knocked mine over."

"Sure," she said, scurrying off to get me one.

I looked over at Horace. Apparently, the cool dip in the pool had done little to sober up the ungrateful lout.

Patricia returned with my drink, a good half of which I downed with one gulp. After making sure Horace was okay, leaving him to sleep it off on the lounger, Patricia approached me again with tears still in her eyes.

"Bless you, Woody. You're a good man. I don't even want to think about what might have happened had you not been here," she said, drying her eyes.

I felt terrible for the poor woman. She was so nice, and he was such a boob.

Patricia tended to Horace while I toweled down. She returned and suggested I get out of my wet clothes for her to throw in the dryer. Showing me inside, she provided a terry bathrobe. I went into the washroom and changed into the robe. While in there, I noticed a hairbrush with some dark brown hair strands in it, a far cry from Patricia's auburn hair. I wondered if it belonged to her housekeeper. When I stepped out of the washroom, I had to ask.

"Is it your housekeeper's day off?" I said.

"We no longer have one," said Patricia. "We couldn't afford her."

I gave her my wet duds, toweled off my hair, and went back outside. I finished my sandwich while waiting for my clothes. Horace was stirring in the lounger, but still quite out of it.

"How are you holding up?" I said to Patricia upon her return.

"I'm so upset. Things have to change. See how nervous I am?" she said, holding out her hands to show how they shook.

"I'm sure things will get better," I said, taking her hands in mine.

There were several moments of silence before either of us spoke again. She pulled her hands away and wiped her eyes. "So how goes the investigation?" she said.

It seemed an abrupt change of subject, but I went with the flow.

"Slowly, but it's still early going! Did anything unusual happen the night the wine went missing?"

"Nothing."

"Did you happen to hear any footsteps going down to the basement during dinner?" I said.

"No, nothing!"

"What about the staff? Does your brother really know them?"

"I believe James had them all looked into before he hired them," she said. "Some have been with him for years."

"Could any of your brother's business associates have it in for him?" I said.

"Woody, my brother may be a grape-grower, but he's a businessman first, and a very successful one," said Patricia. "He has had to be hard-nosed, and sometimes ruthless. I dare say there are probably those who are not that fond of him, but I can't think of anyone who would actually steal from him."

I certainly understood what she meant about hard-nosed. Truth be told, I wasn't sure I was that fond of him myself.

Within thirty minutes, my clothes were not only dry, but warm and toasty. I'd had more than enough excitement for one day, and it was barely one o'clock.

Before leaving, I told Patricia she had a beautiful home.

"Why thank you, Woody," she said, surprised.

"I'd love to see the rest of it. Would you like to give me the grand tour?"

She was so taken with my compliment that I don't think she caught on that it was just an excuse to take a look around. After checking that Horace was all right, she guided me through it.

She showed me the kitchen, bedrooms, and basement, but I found nothing unusual. The rest of the house was just as nicely appointed as the open-concept living/dining area.

Once done, I quickly downed the rest of my drink, thanked Patricia for the soaking—or, rather, the hospitality—and headed back to the estate.

Chapter 11

As I turned up the drive to the front of McCall's house, another car pulled up next to mine. It was a black Bentley from the sixties, beautifully maintained. McCall climbed out as the Bentley continued on to the garage. The door automatically opened and the Bentley drove in. I saw a big guy in a uniform come back out for a moment and then go back in. I could only assume it was the chauffeur, Dan Amos.

"So what's happening, Robins?" McCall said in his usual stern manner. "Fill me in."

"I really don't have much yet," I said.

"Look, I'm not paying you for dilly-dallying. I want results."

Geez, he was aggressive. It had barely been twenty-four hours!

"I've got some leads," I said, defensively. What I had was really very little, if anything. "And I do have a couple questions for you, sir."

"Well, what is it?" he said, gruffly.

"Did you have your staff checked out before you hired them?"

"With the exception of Rodrigo, they all came recommended from extremely reliable previous employers," he said. "That was good enough for me."

I was actually surprised he hadn't had them thoroughly checked out, especially with his wealth. I also asked if he had yet received any kind of ransom note, but he said no.

"Did you happen to hear any unaccounted-for footsteps going down to the basement the night in question?"

"Not a thing," he said.

"Emily tells me she has misgivings about your chauffeur."

"Why, because of his looks?" said McCall. "He's a great mechanic, a good driver, and he knows the region like the back of his hand. I don't have a problem with him. Emily just has an overactive imagination."

With that, McCall turned and headed for the house. I stopped him and asked if I could have a list of his business associates and contact info.

"What the hell do you want with that?" He sounded really ticked off.

"Look, Mr. McCall, you asked me to investigate, and that's what I'm doing," I said. "I would be remiss not to look into them."

After a little more back and forth, he finally agreed, saying he would leave the list with Ms. Svenson. As he began to walk away, I stopped him one more time and asked if he had called another security company to come and check out his system, as I had suggested. He simply shook his head and waved me off like I was a fly bothering him, then went into the house. I yelled after him to make sure that, when he did get another security company out to check out the system, they verified that it was not set up for veiling, but I don't think he heard me.

Boy, what a pleasant sort he is, I thought. I sighed. *I'd better have something substantial to tell him next time, or I might be out of a job.* But when I told him I didn't have much, I wasn't lying. Though I mistrusted Lambeck, not with standing unaccounted-for footsteps the night the wine went missing, and despite the good possibility of sabotage of the vault security system and a poster explaining how to read a French wine label in Rodrigo's apartment, they were all just pieces of a puzzle that might or might not fall into place.

I headed over toward the garage. As I approached, I heard some tinkering and, surprisingly, some classical music—it sounded like Vivaldi's *The Four Seasons*. When I got to the open garage door, there within was the Bentley, a man's legs dangling out from underneath it. Assuming it was Amos, I called out his name, but got no reaction. I stepped up to his legs and gave one of them a light kick.

Immediately, the legs and the rest of the guy they were attached to rolled out on a dolly from under the car.

"What's the problem?" the guy muttered as he got to his feet and turned down the radio.

Built like the proverbial brick house, he was a monster of a man, completely bald, with no neck to speak of. His chest was a wall, his forearms like lampposts, and his legs thick as tree trunks. He had to be six and a half feet tall, and he towered over me.

As I looked at his clean-shaven head, with beady little brown eyes that never seemed to stay still, I could see what Emily meant about his image and demeanor. I didn't get the guilty expression she had mentioned, though—more of a dense sneer.

"I'm Woody Robins," I said, a little intimidated by his stature. "I'm looking into the disappearance of—"

"Yeah, the boss mentioned somethin' 'bout a wine," he said, cutting me off. "You the guy drivin' that yellow 'Vette?"

I had specifically told McCall not to tell any staff members the reason for my questions. Rossi and Lambeck didn't know, so obviously McCall had listened and not told them. Why would he tell only Amos? Maybe, in fact, he hadn't.

"That's me," I said, nodding.

"Your car's making a funny noise." I hadn't noticed. "It sounds like you need a valve adjusted. Bring it around sometime and I'll adjust it for you. It'll only take a couple minutes."

"Thanks. Maybe I will," I said. "So, were you working the night the wine went missing?"

"You a cop?"

"No."

"Then why should I answer your question?"

"Because your boss would like you to cooperate," I said, a little confused at his reluctance.

After a moment of silence, Amos replied: "I was off that night because the boss was staying in with company."

"Do you ever go into the house, Mr. Amos?" I said.

"Only to pick up something from the front hall to put in the car, or to help Ms. Svenson with the groceries."

"That's it?"

"Did you not hear me?" Amos glared at me with those beady eyes.

"So Ms. Svenson never asks you to help carry something down to the basement?"

"You don't listen very well, do you?" He was starting to scare me.

"Are you a wine drinker, Mr. Amos?" I said, changing the subject.

"Wine? I'm a beer guy. Wine is for sissies."

I wasn't about to argue with him. I asked if he knew whether McCall had a wine collection. He said he knew nothing about a wine collection, only that one bottle had been stolen—and, frankly, he didn't care.

"Okay, Mr. Amos," I said, somewhat frustrated. "I think that's all for now."

"Emily doesn't like me, does she?"

"Sorry?" I said, taken aback.

"Emily, one of the boss's daughters, doesn't like me," he said.

"What makes you think that?" I said, pretending it was news to me.

"Just the way she looks at me. And I know she's complained about me to her father."

"Who told you that?"

"I just know," he said. "She's trying to get me fired."

"I'm afraid I know nothing about that," I lied. "Do you mind if I take a look around the garage?"

"Suit yourself," he said as he turned the music back up, got back down on the dolly, and slid under the car.

I would hate to get on his bad side. Amos didn't strike me as a thief, though, least of all for something only "sissies" drink, but stranger things have happened. And talk about strange! The guy appreciated classical music. From his looks, you'd never guess that.

His concern about Emily not liking him, though, seemed out of character. He didn't strike me as the sort who would give a damn whether he was liked or not. Even though he was probably just worried about his job, it seemed odd.

As I pondered, I strolled around the huge car park. There were five other vehicles in there besides the Bentley—a beautifully restored Stutz Bearcat, an older, pristine Rolls, a late-model touring Beamer, a Hummer, and a mint 1950-something Volkswagen Karmann Guia. I assumed the Hummer belonged to Amos.

Although McCall had said there was no other entrance down into the basement of the house, I looked for one anyway, because the garage would be a great place from which to enter and exit the house without actually being seen. In my mind, there had to be another way of getting in and out of the house. This was one of the most important and puzzling aspects of the theft.

However, I found nothing. In one corner of the garage, however, I did find an old tin can that someone had been using as an ashtray, and lying in the bottom were a couple of wine corks. Did they belong to Amos? I could smell cigarette smoke on him, so I assumed he was a smoker, but he said he wasn't a wine drinker. I contemplated asking him about it, but truthfully, after his reaction to my other questions, I was afraid to. I filed that bit of info away for future consideration.

Just then, my cell rang. It was my Aunt Sadie, sounding a little agitated.

"Is everything okay?" I said, concerned.

"My hip is bugging me," she said, "but I'm fine."

She asked if there was more food for Mouton anywhere in the house, because the container in the kitchen was empty. I told her it was down in the basement in the pantry on the second shelf as you walk in the door, and that I would be home later in the day.

After I hung up, I thought I might use the opportunity to call Julia and see how she was doing. She didn't answer, so I left a message on her voice mail.

"From what I understand, Ms. Svenson, you're the only person other than Mr. McCall who has a key to the wine cellar and who actually knows how to get into the private vault," I said. "Is that correct?" I twisted the truth a little to see where it got me.

"I have a key to the wine cellar, but I don't know the code to the vault," Ms. Svenson said. "That's strictly Mr. McCall's domain."

Ms. Svenson had finally agreed to talk. We were sitting in the living room, a grand place with a large stone fireplace, two large columns on both sides of the hearth, and oversized antique furnishings, like three huge camelback couches, numerous easy chairs, and ornamental statues. There were several oriental rugs placed strategically around the space. Fresh flowers adorned the coffee table and several side tables. Above the mantelpiece was a huge oil painting of two gentlemen, one older than the other—McCall's father and grandfather, probably. The resemblance was uncanny. Both possessed those piercing blue eyes.

"Did you have to go down to the wine cellar that evening to choose wine for dinner?" I said to Ms. Svenson, shifting in my seat.

"No, I did that two days before."

"Mr. Lambeck said he heard some footsteps going down to the basement during dinner," I said. "Did you?"

"No," said Ms. Svenson.

"In fact, Mr. Lambeck seems to think you spend an inordinate amount of time down in the wine cellar," I said, twisting the truth again.

"What does that idiot know?" she said, looking irritated. I must have pushed a button.

"I gather you and Mr. Lambeck don't get along," I said.

"He's a miserable stuffed shirt," Ms. Svenson said. "Doesn't like the fact that I'm in charge of the household. Can't handle taking orders from a woman! Thinks he should be running things. I never liked him from day one. I don't trust him. I don't trust Amos, either."

I was certainly with Ms. Svenson about Lambeck, but I was surprised to hear her unprompted comment about the chauffeur. Although he was scary-looking, I didn't really see Amos as a thief. I'd still planned to look into his background, and since Emily and Svenson both had misgivings, I would have to make that a priority.

"Roberto told me that if he needs more wine, either you or Mr. Lambeck retrieves it for him. Is that true?"

"Rossi is mistaken or confused," she said as a matter of fact. "I may have occasionally passed wine onto Lambeck to give to him, but Lambeck never goes into the wine cellar."

"Mr. McCall said that you took a year off from working here to go home," I said. "May I ask why?" I leaned forward in my seat.

"A personal family matter," she said, and that was all.

So I changed direction. "Ms. Svenson, you've been with Mr. McCall a long time now, and you knew his wife. What kind of a person was she?" I said.

She looked at me funny.

"What relevance could that possibly have to the theft?" she said.

"I'm just curious."

"She was nice," she said.

"Did you get along with her okay?"

"Yes," was her answer. I expected her to expand a bit, but she added nothing.

"Look, Mr. Robins," Ms. Svenson said suddenly, "I have some chores that need tending to immediately, so if you don't mind, I'll be moving along."

I was a little miffed at her quick dismissal, but before she left, I asked if I could see her room. She argued a little, as she insisted again that she had chores that needed to be undertaken promptly, but I insisted, so she reluctantly agreed.

Svenson's room was as large as Lambeck's with the same basic layout and furnishings. Gentler colors, a couple bouquets of flowers, and family photos softened the motif. A computer and printer sat on a desk off to one corner. I looked around briefly and superficially, but there was no bottle. It was the best I could do, as she stood over me the whole time shuffling from foot to foot, looking at her watch. Outside in the hall after locking her door, she excused herself, passed me the list of business associates I had requested from McCall, and ran off. I saw her enter the washroom.

From there, I went in search of the boss to tell him I would be going back to San Francisco. Maybe he could provide me contact info for his lawyer, Ralph Wader, and Sam Spezzo, his friend, both of whom lived in the big city. Emily had said that Johnny Spezzo lived at home with his parents, so I would chat with him as well.

As I searched the second floor for McCall, I passed Lambeck's room. I overheard a man's voice—but it wasn't his. It was a New York-type accent. There was no other voice in the conversation, so I just figured Lambeck was on a break, maybe watching some TV where the guy was talking on the phone or something.

After that, I found McCall and told him I was leaving. But when I returned to the cottage to pick up my things, I found a note slipped under the door.

CHAPTER 12

The computer-printed note simply read, "Back off."

Opening the front door again and stepping out, I looked around to see if anyone was about, but there was no one. It worried me. Someone was trying to scare me off. But who? I had no idea. Both Lambeck and Svenson at the house, whose rooms I had searched, had a printer, so it could be either one of them, or someone else entirely.

I left the key on the kitchen counter, grabbed my stuff, and jumped in the car. On my way out to the gates, I passed the stables, where I spotted Denise leading a horse into the barn. I decided to stop and ask some questions.

I found her in one of the stalls, brushing down the mare. She was incredibly gentle with the beast. I watched her for a minute before making my presence known.

"Nice-looking animal," I said, approaching her.

"Yeah," she said, looking up. "She's a beauty. Fast as the wind."

"You really like horses, don't you?"

"They're loyal and trustworthy, and don't put on airs, which is more than I can say about some people."

I made some idle chat about her riding, asking how long she had been doing it. She told that it had been a passion of hers since childhood, and that she belonged to an equestrian club and rode competitively. I remembered her mentioning some competition when she, Emily, and McCall were arguing about money over dinner.

"Denise, have I said or done something to make you dislike me?" I said, moving closer and giving the horse a pat. From the moment I met her, she was standoffish and cold.

"Look, Mr. Robins," she said, putting down her brush. "You haven't said or done anything, and I have nothing against you personally. It's my sister I have a problem with, and it washes over onto others she associates with. She seems to like you, so—"

"Whoa! Where do you get that from? She has a boyfriend she's very much in love with," I said.

"The way she was playing up to you at dinner . . . It made me sick."

"I think she was just being sociable," I said.

Denise just gave me a look that said, "Yeah, right."

Did I detect some jealousy there? I decided not to pursue that any further and asked Denise about the night the wine went missing, but like everyone else, she hadn't seen or heard anything unusual, nor had she heard any footsteps going down to the basement.

"Is there anyone on staff who might have a grudge against your father?" I said.

She stopped what she was doing and thought for a moment.

"No. Father treats all the staff well and pays them decent money," Denise said, continuing to brush the horse.

"What about Dan Amos?" I said. "Your sister seems to think he's trouble."

She threw the brush down and put her hands on her hips.

"My sister is a pain and knows nothing. He's fine. In fact, I find him quite helpful," Denise said.

I was surprised at her reaction. Both Emily and Svenson had misgivings about Amos, but not Denise.

"What do you think of Johnny Spezzo?" I said.

"Not much of anything, except that, because he's involved with Emily, I'm not thrilled with him."

Sort of the same criteria she explained for not particularly liking me, I thought.

"Does he spend much time around the estate?"

"Here's here quite often," she said.

On the surface, it seemed the relationship between Denise and Emily was like that between many siblings. Being an only child, I didn't know this first-hand, but many friends had relayed stories of sibling rivalry over relative successes, parental affection, and relationship jealousy.

"Does it bother you that your sister has a boyfriend and you don't?" I said, knowing I would get a reaction.

"What the hell are you getting at?" she said, again stopping her brushing and glaring at me.

I ignored her question and asked another: "Do you have any guy friends who come around the house?"

"My personal life is none of your business, Mr. Robins."

"Sorry," I said, putting my hands in the air. "I'm just doing my job."

"I know what you're doing," she said. "It's called snooping."

"That's what investigators do, Denise."

"You're not an investigator. You're a wine guy."

"Yeah—a wine guy hired by your father to investigate!"

"Don't care!" she said, quite smugly.

"At some point, I *would* like to have a look around your room."

"Like hell you will!" she said, almost barking at me.

So much for that! I thanked her for her time and handed her one of my cards just in case she remembered anything about that night she might have forgotten to tell me. She took the card, threw it on a stack of hay next to the stall, and went back to grooming the horse. As I turned to leave, she said one more thing: "Keep an eye out. Many folks around here aren't all they appear to be."

During the drive back to San Francisco, I recorded some more notes on my tape recorder, easy to do mostly hands-free. I had a few solid leads and a lot of questions and contradictions. On the machine, I had previously noted Emily's problems with her father for not paying for her education. I could tell she was also awfully mad at him about her mother's illness. She had been about to say something about it, but stopped herself.

I added other tidbits on the drive, like the visits to Rodrigo's place and Patricia and Horace's house, and the conversations with Amos, Svenson, and Denise. I also noted the fact that Emily seemed quite interested in me—at least according to her sister—even though she had a boyfriend! And he, Johnny Spezzo, didn't seem jealous at all.

Rossi, the chef, had said both Svenson and Lambeck retrieved wine for him, but Svenson said only she actually retrieved it from the wine cellar. Lambeck denied handling wine at all. Svenson was also intriguing about McCall and his wife. As for Patricia, she implied that she and Horace were in need of money because of Horace's poor business savvy—so much so that they had to release their housekeeper. A very strange development—she came from a wealthy family. She said McCall had all his staff checked out before he hired them, but he said otherwise.

Why McCall would tell Amos in particular the reason for my questioning when I specifically asked him not to—especially given he hadn't told his other staff—was a mystery. Amos was also aware that Emily didn't like him, and even though he said "wine is for sissies," there were wine corks in his ashtray. Denise found the guy "helpful," and seemed offended by Emily's insinuations otherwise. She didn't want me to look in her room, either. Was she hiding something?

No one other than Lambeck had heard the so-called footsteps on the stairs going down to the basement that night. Johnny Spezzo and Touchstone seemed to be, at least on paper, the perfect team to effectively sabotage a security system, especially given their expertise in the army. And someone was trying to scare me off.

While driving along, I placed a call to a buddy of mine—George Gold, a homicide detective with the San Francisco police force. Georgey, as I call him, has been a pal since high school, back when he was a fun-loving, devil-may-care kind of guy. After graduation, he pursued his lifelong dream of becoming a cop, slowly working his way up the ranks.

At a glance, he didn't really look like a cop. With thinning red hair, a pencil-thin moustache, and glasses, he looked more like an accountant. I asked if he could possibly do a background check on Ms. Svenson, Dan Amos, Horace Botner, Michael Lambeck, and Johnny Spezzo.

"What's the matter, Woody?" he said. "These folks not playing nice?"

Georgey came off as a bit gruff at times—a bit of a slob, too—but he was a real stand-up guy when you needed him, and he had a mind like a steel trap. He also had a huge secret that very few people other than myself knew—the guy loved comic books, and had an incredible collection of one-of-a-kind, original, mint editions. Whenever he got the chance, he'd sneak off to comic book stores in the city to rifle through the books, looking for new rare additions to his collection. He even frequented Comic-Con every year in San Diego, and dressed up in costume. The guy is a real nerd that way.

"If you help me, I've got a beautiful '97 Brunello di Montalcino with your name on it," I said.

Georgey was a recent convert to wine, but he loved the stuff, especially reds from Tuscany. Over the years, I'd called upon him to obtain certain information, and in return, I passed on to him advice on what wines to buy, threw some bottles his way, and occasionally got him invited to wine events like tastings, winemaker dinners, festivals, and trade shows.

"Look, kiddo," said Georgey, "as much as I'd like to help you out, and that wine does sound great, I'm up to my ears in work here. Besides, it's not official police business. Sorry!"

Rats, I thought.

Hanging up with Georgey, I realized I'd have to look into these people myself.

It was about 3 p.m. when I got back to San Francisco. The traffic was a bit slow up to Oakland, but the pace picked up as I approached the Bay Bridge. Before too long, I was pulling into my driveway.

I was lucky enough to possess one of the few bungalows in North Beach. Land here is at a real premium, the majority of dwellings built upward as opposed to outward, so most properties are the size of postage stamps.

North Beach is a colorful part of the city, loved by both tourists and locals. Perhaps it helps that it's San Fran's Little Italy. The neighborhood is just teeming with Italian flavor: Michelangelo Cafe, Calzone's and many other restaurants, cafés, clubs, bars, etc. Even some great delis are here. And always lots of action!

As soon as my key was in the front door, I heard meowing on the other side. I opened the door to find Mouton whining away, ticked at me for leaving her. Although I knew Sadie had stopped by and seen to her needs, it wasn't the same. She wasn't Daddy.

"Hello, baby. Daddy's home," I said, putting my bag down and cuddling her. She immediately flopped down on her back, presenting her belly for rubbing. Several minutes of attention and she was satisfied, allowing me to carry on, but she followed me around just in case I made any moves to leave again.

The place looked fine. I went into the office and dropped my briefcase. There were twelve messages on the answering machine, but I would deal with them later. Continuing on to the smallish galley kitchen, I spotted a bag and a note on the counter. From the smell, I could tell Sadie had left me some bagels from the Bagelry. Bless her heart. The Jewish deli and bakery in the Russian Hill part of town makes the best bagels on the planet.

The note simply said, "Welcome home. Mouton is fine, but misses Daddy. Call me. Love, S."

Before I could start in doing some background checks on my suspects, I had other work to catch up on. I prepared my notes for my wine appreciation class the next morning at 10:30 at Rosewell College and jotted down some initial notes for another one of my columns that was due by the end of the week. One of the messages on my answering machine was a guy who wanted me to do an appraisal. I prepared an appraisal agreement and sent it off. By the time I was caught up, it was early evening. I toasted one of the bagels Sadie had left me and scrambled some eggs. A glass of orange juice with ice washed it down. It was simple but satisfying.

After dinner, I looked into McCall's business associates, which included many wine producers. Finding nothing of any significance, I called it a night. While in bed, I dialed Julia to let her know I was home. She sounded sleepy.

"Did I wake you, hon?" I said.

"Oh, Woody, it's been crazy busy at work. I must have dozed off. Are you at home?"

"Just got in a few hours ago. And if you're not busy on Saturday, why don't you come over for dinner? I'll cook."

There was silence for a moment.

"Sounds great. Looking forward to it," she said. "Can I bring anything?"

"Just your lovely, sexy self," I said. She giggled. "Shall we say about six?"

"Six it is. Love you, hon, and sleep tight."

"Right back at ya! Goodnight," I said, then hung up. I was relieved she didn't bring up the moving-in thing again, though I was pretty sure it wouldn't be ignored Saturday night.

CHAPTER 13

The next morning, after rising early and taking a quick shower, I spent my time before class on the computer, looking into some of my suspects. First, I punched in "Dan Amos," but came up dry. I tried all kinds of tangents, such as "chauffeurs," "drivers," "mechanics," etc., but none brought any concrete results. To be sure, a more hands-on approach might yield something. Maybe I could tail him sometime and see.

Next, I keyed in "Michael Lambeck." Again, I got nothing. But what was the name of the club he worked at in New York before coming to Napa? I racked my brain but couldn't pull it out.

Then, I remembered I had noted the name in one of my recordings. I looked in my briefcase, but my tape recorder wasn't there. Remembering I had done some recording while driving home from McCall's, I went out to the car to look for it. It wasn't there, either.

Crap, I thought. *Where the hell is it?*

I tore the car apart looking for it, but came up empty. Then I ran into the house, frantically retracing my steps from the previous day, but again, nothing. Going back into the office, I scoured it thoroughly, but no luck.

"Damn!" I said, banging my hand down on the desk. What was I going to do now? There were so many important notes about this case on that recording. I couldn't possibly remember them all. I prayed it would turn up at some point.

Frustrated as I was, I continued to search the net, but kept ending up at dead ends. But then—something really mind-boggling!

In one of my searches, I spelled Lambeck's name wrong and, as search engines often do, it asked me if I meant something else: "Lambini." Just out of curiosity, I clicked on that, and it took me to an interesting link. It talked about some Brooklyn, New York native by the name of Mitch

"Mickey" Lambini, a small-time racketeer, hood, and two-bit actor connected to the Genovese Family, one of the five remaining New York crime families. Finding it fascinating, I kept pursuing this character . . . then, bingo. One of the links showed a photo of this guy.

"Holy crap!" I squealed, just about falling off my chair.

Staring back at me from the computer screen was Michael Lambeck, alias Mitch "Mickey" Lambini. Despite Lambini's beard, there was no mistaking the eyebrows. Then it dawned on me: The voice I had heard outside Lambeck's room while seeking out the second floor washroom wasn't the TV at all, but most probably his. The guy was a complete fraud.

I sat there in astonishment for several moments. Obviously, McCall didn't know.

After the shock of my discovery wore off, I tried to think about this logically. Should I inform McCall? Who and what Lambeck was would make him a prime suspect in the wine's theft, but it didn't prove he was involved. If he *was* involved, then maybe this case stretched much further than I had anticipated—that is, to the mob. But if he was *not* involved, then why was he playing an English butler?

I reached for my tape recorder to note this, but then realized again that I didn't have it. *Crap!*

I decided to keep this quiet for a while and see how it played out. If he wasn't involved in the theft, I didn't want it to impede the investigation.

Next, I tried "Horace Botner." Several links appeared. I first checked out the one from Speedy Cleaners, his defunct cleaning business. I learned how he had taken a small, failing cleaning business and turned it into a multi-million-dollar enterprise with eight locations across the state. Twice during his heyday, he was named entrepreneur of the year in *Businessweek* magazine. *Newsweek* had actually done a huge spread on him.

According to the *Newsweek* article, Horace was born to a piss poor family in Los Angeles. His older brother had died before Horace was twenty. It took great conviction and work to put himself through school before buying into the cleaning business. He'd met Patricia at a country club soiree on a trip out to wine country in Napa to open another branch. Two years later, they were married. They had one child, a daughter, who moved to England. From all accounts, the guy was a winner and a very successful self-made businessman. So what happened?

Another piece in *The San Francisco Chronicle*, dated November 9, 2004, answered the question. Horace lost the business in a card game, of all things. That was interesting—Patricia had said it was a bad investment.

Probably just too embarrassed to be truthful, I thought. So it would seem that Horace had a serious gambling problem, which cost him his livelihood. His subsequent failures, as Patricia put it, were probably due to lack of funds.

Then I realized why the Botners were short on cash, even though Patricia was from a wealthy family: Horace had probably gambled a good portion of it away. I supposed he kept thinking he could somehow win enough money back to re-establish himself. It never seemed to happen, so he turned to alcohol to numb the pain. *The guy has a sickness all right,* I thought. *No wonder he's so broken.* Still, I wondered why Patricia didn't just ask her brother for some help.

Lack of funds was certainly enough motive for Horace to steal the wine and sell it, especially if he owed money from a gambling debt. As to whether he actually did the deed, I couldn't say.

There was something related I felt was important here, but I couldn't remember it for the life of me. No matter how hard I searched my memory, it was no use. I was sure I had noted it in one of my recordings.

Looking at my watch, I realized I was running late and got myself together to get to the college. On the drive down, I called Charlie to see if he was available after class for lunch at the Gull to see what he had come up with from his net search. He agreed.

Class went well. I lectured on the idea of wine as an investment—a compelling concept if I have to say so myself. Arriving at the Gull after class, I noticed the outdoor patio was jammed—and inside, too. But I spotted Charlie at my favorite table in the corner and headed over in his direction.

The C-Gull, or "Gull," as the locals call it, is an interesting establishment. It occupies a prime southeast corner about three blocks southwest of my street, right in the heart of North Beach. Three local siblings from the Conway family bought it about five years ago.

The restaurant's interior is decorated, in a very "yo ho ho" style, with all sorts of nautical paraphernalia. Along one side, over the forty-five foot, solid mahogany bar—actually absconded from an old merchant ship—are all manner of fishing gear, tackle, ship ornaments, foghorns, harpoons, life preservers, and whatnots. Twenty-five round wooden tables, tastefully covered in blue-and-white-checkered tablecloths and ships lanterns, fill up the cozy space. Another ten tables occupy the outdoor patio that spills out onto the side street and Grant Avenue. The walls drip with old sea maps, fishing nets, and portholes. Antique ship lamps hang from the rafters. Off to one side, near the bar, is a small stage, affectionately called the "Poop Deck," where light jazz trios and ensembles play on Friday and Saturday nights.

Perhaps the most intriguing thing about the place is its name. It existed previously as the Seagull. The Conways, not really wanting to change a landmark of two decades, kept the name but changed the "Sea" to "C." Pretty ingenious, huh?

Aside from frequenting one of my favorite eateries and watering holes, I regularly consulted for the place, handling staff training and updating their wine list.

Charlie was so busy chatting up some pretty young thing at the table next to him that he didn't even notice my arrival. His white, slightly wrinkled cotton jersey and beige cargo pants made it look as if he had slept in his clothes. It was a wonder Charlie, who fell over himself with awkward verbosity, could score with any babes, but strangely enough, he did pretty well in that area. It had to be the doe-eyed Bambi look and the blond hair.

Finally, he turned around.

"Who the hell dressed you today, dude—Butch Cassidy or the Sundance Kid?" Charlie said, eyeing me from stem to stern.

Dressed in a pair of light, pleated, cranberry-colored linen trousers with a beige weaved belt, short-sleeved, button-down, navy-blue shirt, café mocha-colored vest, tan leather boat shoes, no socks, and a twilled, wine-colored cap with snap-down brim right out of the Bowery Boys, I had no idea what he was talking about. I thought I looked quite dashing.

Just then, Sue, the manager, came waltzing over, looking fabulous in a pair of Levis and a red T-shirt.

"Ah, Sue, my darling," I said, taking her hand in mine. "Come fly with me. Let me whisk you away from all this."

"No way! I never fly with a guy who dresses like you do." She pulled her hand back. "What's your tipple, Woody?"

Sitting down, I asked Charlie what he was sipping. He had a Vodka on the rocks with a twist, so I ordered one, another for my comrade, and lunch.

"Notice anything different about me, Woody?" Charlie said.

Looking him over, I confessed I didn't.

"It's on my face, guy," he said, pushing his kisser forward.

I still didn't see anything different.

"My upper lip, Hershey!"

"Don't call me that," I said, angrily. When, years ago, he found out about my middle moniker, Hershel—given to me by my great-grand-father—which I despise and never use, he started calling me Hershey whenever possible, just to piss me off.

"Actually, yeah!" I said, pointing at his upper lip. "You got a bit of a dirty smudge there."

"Don't be lame. It's not a smudge. I'm sprouting a moustache," he said, stroking it with his finger.

"Well, it looks like dirt to me," I said. With his fair hair, it wasn't noticeable at all.

At that point, Sue returned with our drinks. I took a quick sip. *Refreshing!*

"So tell me," I said to Charlie, leaning back in my chair. "What, if anything, did you find out?"

"I gotta tell ya, man, that was a miserable, long, tedious job," he said.

"I told you, Sherlock—investigation isn't all fun and games."

Pulling out a list from one of the snap pockets on his pants, he started in. He told me several agents had wines: some '61 red Bordeaux, '49 red Burgundies, '55 Sauternes, and '52 red Rhônes.

"Nothing older?" I said.

"That's it, dude," he said, folding up the piece of paper. "Took me four and half hours. Oh yeah, one agent said there was a rumor floating around about a rare bottle that might be available, but they couldn't say what or when."

"Who was the agent?" I said, leaning forward.

Opening up the paper again and looking through the list of contacts, he told me it was Rainbow Imports. I wrote down the number on a napkin and stuffed it in my pocket.

"You done good, Charlie," I said. "Hey, you do a lot of deliveries for Barnes & Dexter in the area, don't you?"

"You mean that law firm near the corner of Columbus and Broadway?"

"That's the one," I said, nodding.

"Not anymore. We lost that account. Why?"

I had meant to ask him to check if the lawyers in that company knew anything about McCall's lawyer, Ralph Wader. Perhaps they knew each as members of the Bar.

"Doesn't matter now," I said.

Just then, our lunch arrived: thinly-sliced, rare, roast beef piled high with tomatoes and lettuce, between two slices of dark rye with seeds, lathered with spicy, brown mustard. On the side, the Gull's famous homemade potato salad and a kosher dill! We spent the next half hour or so eating, drinking, and yakking about other stuff. When complete and satiated, I paid the bill and each of us went our merry way.

CHAPTER 14

During the drive home, my cell phone rang. It was Sadie.

"Are you okay?" I said.

She said she was fine, but needed to talk. She asked if I could meet her for a coffee. We agreed to meet in about twenty minutes at the Starbucks near her place. I arrived before she and sat at a small table by the window, a coffee in hand. Within a few minutes, her Lexus pulled up and she got out, hobbling. Entering the Starbucks, she gave me a peck on the cheek and sat down, looking as if she was in a lot of pain. I got up and ordered her a coffee.

"The hip's worse, isn't it?" I said when I returned, watching her grimace.

"It's fine," she said, brushing it off.

"So what's this all about then?" I said, taking a sip of my coffee.

"Try not to get too upset with what I'm about to tell you," said Sadie, "but I thought you should hear it from me, instead of finding out some other way."

I started to feel sick. When someone starts a conversation like that, one usually expects the worst.

"Okay," I said apprehensively.

"When I was out yesterday around midday, running some errands close to where Julia works, I spotted her at an outdoor café, lunching with some guy. They were holding hands."

My heart sank.

"I don't know what it meant," she said. "But they looked cozy."

I sat there in silence, thinking about what I had just been told. I knew I was having trouble committing to living with Julia and she had said that she wasn't going to hang around forever, but I didn't think for one minute that she was looking around already, especially while we were still together. She said she loved me.

"Do you know who the guy was?" I said.

"No. I'm so sorry, Woody."

"Maybe it's innocent. A relative?" I was clutching at straws.

"Perhaps, Woody, but one usually doesn't hold hands with a relative," she said.

I stared down in my coffee and felt ill.

"You okay?" she said, pulling her chair up next to mine and putting her arm around me.

I just nodded. I felt like crying, but held myself back.

"It's not too late, Woody. You can still save this relationship," she said, pulling me closer.

We sat there for another ten minutes or so, finishing our coffee while Sadie consoled me. I then told her I had to leave. I helped Sadie to her car and kissed her on the cheek. Just before she drove away, she told me she loved me.

The drive home was painful. It was true—I probably could still save the relationship. However, I didn't want to be forced or pressured into making the big move out of jealousy.

When I got home, there was more bad news. A message from McCall on my office phone told me Horace had been beaten up real bad. He was in the hospital, and in a coma. I quickly dialed McCall. He wasn't at home, but Ms. Svenson gave me his cell number.

"Any idea who did it?" I said when I reached him.

"No clue," McCall said, sounding very concerned.

Horace had been in town when it happened, and was brought to San Francisco General, not far from my home, at around 10 a.m. that morning. I figured I'd take a run over there to see if there was anything I could do to help. When I arrived, I found that Horace had been moved to a private room on the fourth floor. I found Patricia and McCall outside his room. Patricia was crying.

"How's he doing?" I said, putting my hand on Patricia's shoulder.

"He's in rough shape. The doctors can't or won't say anything more," McCall said.

"Any idea who could have done this to him?" I said.

McCall couldn't answer the question, and Patricia couldn't stop crying long enough to try.

I looked through the little glass window into Horace's room. He was taped up and cast like a mummy, black and blue, hooked to machines with wires and hoses. A doctor was in there with him. Telling McCall I'd check in later to see how Horace was doing, I left the hospital and headed home. Although I felt sorry for Horace and Patricia, I felt worse for myself.

Once back at the house, I didn't really feel like doing anything except moping. But realizing that that wouldn't change a thing with Julia, I threw myself back into the case. At least that would take my mind off her. I decided to call the wine agent Charlie had mentioned. I pulled out of my pocket the napkin on which I had written down the info, but do you think I could read my own writing?

Damn and blast, I thought. I had to call Charlie back to get the info again.

When I finally reached the agent at Rainbow Imports, they said they had heard about the bottle from another agent at Calder Wine & Spirits. They, in turn, informed me they had heard it from Trillium International. Calling the third agent got me results. However, the wine in question ended up being a large bottle of old, vintage Champagne, not a red Burgundy.

So where else would someone go to sell a rare, precious wine? *Perhaps a wine shop*, I thought. I had planned on asking Julia about that earlier, but had not gotten around to it, and now this new information from Sadie made it all seem somehow less important. So where else?

An auction house would not be bad, but it would most definitely draw attention to the crime. However, I needed to cover all my bases, so I would have to check them anyway. I knew that not all auction houses dealt with wine. Through Google, I came up with three in the Bay area that did: Greg Martin Auctions on Bryant Street, Wine Gavel Fine and Rare Wine Auctions on California Street, and Bonham & Butterfields on San Bruno Avenue. Scribbling down the addresses on a piece of paper, I changed into something more sedate. I'd have to look legit. Attired now in a pair of double-pleated, navy blue slacks, a bone-colored, short-sleeve dress shirt, gray single-breasted sport jacket, and black brogues (avec socks), I ventured out. No lid this time!

I visited all three houses and, with the exception of decor and size, they were basically set up the same way. They had bars on the windows, which made them look like swanky pawn shops. You had to be buzzed in by an employee. They all had display cases containing varied collectables, including antique corkscrews, Elizabethan crystal stemware and decanters, silver and gold tastevins, and other ancient, obscure, and, I was sure, expensive wine paraphernalia.

The story I used for all of them was that my sources in France had told me that Napoleon's Burgundy was on the market and being peddled here, instead of in France, for tax reasons. Of course, none of the folks I spoke with believed it even existed, let alone was being sold, so I had to grease their palms a little to keep them interested. I had stopped at the bank on the way down for just this purpose. I laid a fifty on each of them and simply asked that, if they were approached with this item, they'd call me immediately so I'd get first dibs. All three houses agreed, pocketing the money and chuckling with disbelief. It was a long shot, I know, and I didn't really have the bucks to spare, but I figured I'd just add it to McCall's invoice.

Back at the house, I worked on a few things unrelated to the case. But considering Julia, I found it hard to concentrate. She would be coming over the night after next for dinner. I contemplated calling her to cancel, but eventually decided otherwise. *I can overcome this*, I thought. *Maybe I can still see her while she sees other guys.*

Before retiring for the night, I called McCall to see how Horace was doing. There was no change. He also informed me that he finally had another security company come out to look at his system, and they said it checked out fine.

"Did they verify that your system wasn't set up for veiling?" I said.

"What the hell are you talking about?"

He hadn't heard my comment about verifying the veiling theory after all. Or maybe he just chose to ignore it. Who knows?

CHAPTER 15

The next morning, I shopped for tomorrow's dinner.

Then I went to see Ralph Wader. His digs were in the city's financial district, where most banks house their corporate offices in high-rises. Wader's office was on the seventh floor of a tall, swank building right on Montgomery Street. The sign on the shiny brass mantle next to the door read, "Ralph Wader, Attorney at Law." The place was posh on the inside, too: gleaming metal and leather furniture, light pastel-colored walls with tasteful, original watercolors, and pen-and-ink drawings. With several computers, fax machines, copiers, and scanners, it looked like a page right out of *Modern Business* Magazine. When I entered and announced myself to the receptionist, she buzzed Wader, and he promptly appeared.

An average-looking, clean-shaven fellow in his late fifties, with receding, slicked-back brown hair, glasses, and a hearing aid in his left ear, Wader led me into his inner sanctum.

"I've been James's attorney for some eighteen years now," Wader said, sitting down behind his desk. His office carried over the décor of the lobby. "My father was his father's lawyer, so I guess we've known the family a long time."

"It's nice when several generations of a family can maintain the same business relationship with a client, isn't it?"

"Yes, it is. It's been a pleasure representing him all these years," he said.

"So, you'd probably know most of his business associates?" I said.

"I believe so."

"Any of them that you can think of might have it in for him?"

"Not to my knowledge," he said.

"Did you notice anything unusual or suspicious the night the wine went missing?"

"Not a thing," he said, cocking his head to the side and thinking a minute. "It was simply a quiet, pleasant evening, with good conversation and delightful food."

"Now, Mr. Wader—"

"Call me Ralph," he said, crossing his legs.

"Ralph, you knew Mr. McCall owned that bottle of rare wine?" I said.

"Of course I did. James had asked my legal advice about the wine's purchase, transport, and customs issues when he originally decided to buy it. I had advised him against doing so."

I was surprised at the comment. Leaning forward, I asked him if it had anything to do with a curse.

"A *what?*"

"Never mind," I said. "Do you mind if I ask why?"

"It was way too expensive, especially for something that, more than likely, was no longer any good to drink. The French taxes, import duties, shipping, insurance, and paperwork were a phenomenal nightmare. In my mind, it wasn't worth the aggravation.

Don't get me wrong here," he said, leaning forward on his elbows. "I appreciate the sentiment of a gift for his wife and all, but perhaps he could have gotten her something that involved less red tape. Maybe some jewelry!"

"I see," I said. I hadn't realized the wine was a gift for his wife.

Leaning back in his chair, he said, "There's no telling James what to do, though. Once he gets his mind wrapped around an idea, that's it. I guess that's part of what makes him such a successful businessman." He paused. "So tell me—would that bottle still be any good? I mean, it's very old."

"Can't really say, Ralph," I said. "When was the last time you actually saw the wine in person?"

He scratched his head and again took a couple moments to answer.

"Had to have been about a couple weeks earlier," he finally said. "I happened to be over at the house when James had somebody from the security company out for some fine-tuning. James had to remove the bottle while the guy worked," said Wader, "so I saw it then."

Wait a minute, I thought, sitting forward. Joey Touchstone had said she was the only one who serviced her equipment.

"You're sure the security company person was a guy?" I said.

"Of course I'm sure."

"Can you describe the guy?"

"He was a little overweight, in his mid-to-late forties, and swarthy, with a moustache and dark hair. He looked European—maybe Italian," said Wader. "He worked for forty-five minutes, and McCall never left him alone."

Returning to my car, I instinctively reached in my briefcase for my tape recorder, but then remembered, again, that I didn't have it. *Bloody hell!*

So I rummaged through my bag looking for a piece of paper. Don't think for one moment that the idea of this security guy being somehow related to the mob didn't cross my mind. Scribbling down the idea on a piece of paper I found in my briefcase, I stuffed the note in my shirt pocket. Then I pulled out the business card from Touchstone Security. I dialed the number, asking to speak with Joey Touchstone. The receptionist put me on hold, then returned to tell me she wasn't available. I left a message for her to call me back, but I didn't really expect her to. I would try again later.

Since I was out and about, I thought it might not be a bad idea to interview the Spezzos. When I called, Sam Spezzo asked if I could come to the house in Nob Hill within a half hour.

Nob Hill is an upscale San Francisco neighborhood with fantastic vistas of the bay. One look at the large mansions, private clubs, and expensive hotels, and you know there's *mucho* money tied up here.

Working my way over to Powell Street, I found the place without much difficulty and pulled into the driveway. The abode was a grand, three-story affair with leaded, beveled glass windows and at least three chimneys. Knocking on the door, I was greeted by Sam's wife, Lucy, a short, slim, nice-looking woman of about sixty with black hair graying at the temples and an air of sophistication.

"Please come in, Mr. Robins," she said. "Sam is expecting you."

She led me into a sitting room. The interior of the house was all you'd expect: huge rooms and antique furnishings. Buffets, sideboards, china cabinets, commodes, consoles, and parlor tables abounded. There were also a large, studded leather couch, chairs, and plenty of knickknacks. The place smacked of money.

"Ah, Mr. Robins, so nice to meet you," said the man of the house, making his entrance.

About his wife's age, short, solid, and stalky, with sleepy, droopy Paul McCartney eyes and a rosy complexion, he possessed the biggest ears I had ever seen on a human. His earlobes looked like two tremendous slabs of Provimi veal hanging from his head on either side. He stuck out his hand.

I shook it and cringed. His grip was incredibly strong. He just about broke my knuckles. As I'd said before, you can tell a lot about a person by their handshake, but broken bones are another story.

"Thank you for taking the time to see me, Mr. Spezzo," I said. "I appreciate it."

He offered me a seat and a drink.

"Lucy and I were just about to have one," he said, sitting down.

"Whatever you're having is fine, sir."

"Then gin and tonic it is."

As Lucy went over to a side bar and prepared three G and Ts, Sam answered my questions before I even had a chance to ask them.

"I'm afraid there's not much either Lucy or I can tell you," Sam said. "We arrived the day before, after lunch, with our children, and left the morning after the dinner. We heard or saw nothing unusual. It was a typical visit with James."

"I'm sorry," I said. "Did you say children?"

"Yes, my son, Johnny, and my daughter, Maria," he said.

I hadn't been aware they had a daughter, too.

I couldn't help but notice that, every now and then when Sam spoke, he had a bit of a twitch on the left side of his face that caused his head to jerk ever so slightly. He spoke of his family's origins in Sicily, settling in Cambridge, Massachusetts before coming west.

"Mr. Spezzo, how long have you known James McCall?" I said, taking a sip of my drink.

"Some thirty-five years. We met shortly after I got out of the armed forces. The four of us—James, Laura, Lucy, and I—became fast friends when I helped him buy some vineyard land in Napa."

"So sad about Laura—such a dear woman," Lucy said, interjecting. "I miss her immensely. I know it's been hard for James and the girls."

Since she had brought up McCall's wife, Laura, I asked Lucy a few questions about her. Laura, she said, hadn't been sick a day in her life.

Then, all of a sudden, she started to have pain. She was diagnosed with cancer, and within four months, she was gone.

"Emily and Denise don't seem to like each other," I said, swirling the ice in my drink.

"They had already been going at it for years," said Sam. "But when Laura passed away, it got worse." As an interesting aside, Sam informed me that McCall had always wanted a son, and although he loved the girls, he was disappointed that he didn't have someone to carry on the family name.

Since I had them in what seemed like a talkative mood, I decided to ask some questions about Emily's relationship with her father, because she seemed to hold the most animosity toward him.

"Emily basically blamed James for her mother's death—for taking too much time before getting her proper treatment by specialists," Sam said. "I personally don't believe it would have made any difference, but that resentment runs awfully deep. She never forgave him."

At least that somewhat explained Emily's ranting and raving during our walk in the garden. I couldn't help but wonder if that was impetus enough to steal her father's wine—maybe to get back at him somehow. Perhaps she enlisted the help of her boyfriend, who just happened to be a computer expert *and* a friend of the folks who created and installed the security system.

"Emily and Johnny are a couple," I said. "Correct?"

"That's right."

I asked how long they had been going out. Lucy said about a year or so. They had actually known each other most of their lives, but it didn't start getting serious until Emily came home from college. Lucy actually thought they might get married.

"Mr. Spezzo, did you know Mr. McCall had that wine?"

"Sure. He showed it to me several times," Sam said, taking a sip of his drink. "But to be honest, I really don't know why James bought it. He has so much wine, after all—he didn't really need it. He wasn't even planning to drink it. It was just for show. I warned him that something like this might happen if he owned a rare treasure like that."

"Why would you warn him?" I said. "Don't you think he was aware of that?"

"James is a great guy, and an astute businessman," Sam said, "but sometimes, he's a little naïve about his wealth. He likes to think the best of people. Can't fathom someone wanting to do him harm."

That was funny. McCall didn't strike me at all like the type who was naïve about anything. Furthermore, if he wasn't aware that his commanding attitude and aggressive personality might put people off, then he was living in a dream world.

"If you had any suspicions about any of the folks at the dinner," I said, "who would it be?"

As soon as the words left my mouth, Sam's expression changed. He looked as if I had asked something I shouldn't have. I don't know why. Under the circumstances, it was a perfectly legitimate question and simply common sense that someone at the dinner party would have some involvement in the theft.

"I beg your pardon?"

"I'm sorry. Let me put it another way," I said, shifting in my seat.

"Surely you're not implying that family or friends had anything to do with the theft," he said.

"I'd like to think not, sir," I said, "but in cases like this, it's often someone close to the victim."

Getting huffy, Sam dismissed the idea promptly. Somehow, he seemed to take the question personally. Realizing I was perhaps overstaying my welcome, I asked if Johnny was about, but was informed he was out in Napa seeing Emily. I thanked them for their time and the drink.

I shook Sam's hand and found it to be clammy, though his grip was even tighter than before. Maybe the clamminess was due to his blood pressure—or maybe because I had gotten him riled up.

More and more points seemed to support the Italian mob connection theory. I hate to stereotype, but there was not only Lambeck, but also the security guy who might be Italian, the Spezzos—especially Johnny, given his area of expertise—and even Rossi, the chef.

Back home, I searched the Internet for some background on Ralph Wader. I learned that he had graduated magna cum laude from Harvard Law School and was, from all accounts, a well-respected, extremely successful lawyer. As for the Spezzos, Sam was a giant in California real estate. The family's Sicilian heritage was mentioned, but without details. Again, I racked my brain for that little, important tidbit about a possible mob connection I was sure I had noted on my tape recorder, but it just wouldn't come. *Damn! Damn! Damn!*

What to do next? It was early enough to take a trip back out to the estate. I wanted to check out Amos a bit closer, since my net searches had found nothing on him. During the drive, I dialed Touchstone's number again and got the same result. I would be out that way anyway, so I figured I could drop in and address Joey face to face.

Great plan, for sure—but as it turned out, when I got to Napa, she was conveniently out of the office. Whether she actually was or wasn't, she certainly wasn't available for me.

CHAPTER 16

As I was climbing back into my car outside Touchstone's showroom, I heard someone calling my name. When I turned around, there was Emily across the street, looking ravishing in a pair of Calvin Kleins and a T-shirt.

"What are you doing here?" I asked when she came across the street to me.

"I just finished a shift at the drop-in center. Hey, do you have time for a drink, or maybe coffee?"

It was a hot day, so a cool drink sounded like a good idea.

In a nice little bar a block away, we ordered a couple of gin and tonics as we sat and enjoyed the air conditioning.

"So where's Johnny today?" I said, looking around.

"He's in San Francisco. He's coming out later, and we're going out for dinner."

That's interesting. Sam Spezzo had said that Johnny was out in Napa seeing Emily. So where was he? But actually, this might work out well—if indeed Johnny would be around later on, I'd get a chance to question him. He was definitely high on the list of my prime suspects.

Looking at Emily as she spoke, I couldn't get over how beautiful and sexy she was. Johnny was truly a lucky man—and that made me feel that much worse about what was going on with Julia. I was attracted to Emily, and I was riddled with guilt about it. I was heartbroken about Julia possibly starting to see other guys, but couldn't commit to her. Boy, was I confused.

As we sat, sipping our drinks and chatting, I looked toward the front window.

Johnny Spezzo stared back at us with a big grin on his face.

When I looked again, he was gone. *Spooksville for sure!*

"Are you sure Johnny's in San Francisco?" I said, squirming in my seat.

"Absolutely. I spoke to him not a half hour ago." Emily looked at me funny.

We continued to chat, especially about Horace. When I asked how he was doing, she said he was still the same—no improvement. If he recovered, it would take some time. Once again, I questioned the possibility of his involvement in the theft. Her answer this time was odd.

"I really don't think my uncle has the wits to pull off something like that," she said.

For a guy who took a failing business and turned it into an empire, wits didn't seem to be an issue.

"So what about you, Woody? Is there a Mrs. Robins? I didn't notice a wedding ring," Emily said, examining my hand.

"Actually, I have a beautiful, long-haired lady who lives with me in San Francisco."

"Oh?" she said, looking maybe a little disappointed.

"Yeah," I said. "She has four legs and uses a litter box."

"You have a cat?" Emily said, a surprised look on her face.

"She's more than a cat. She's a precious little ball of lovable fur," I said. "Her name is Mouton. She—"

And then I saw Johnny again, grinning away through the front window. It freaked me out and I shifted nervously in my seat. When I looked again . . . nothing.

"What is the matter with you?" Emily said, starting to look concerned.

"Are you absolutely sure Johnny's in San Fran?" I said.

"Yes," she said, getting a bit exasperated.

We quickly finished our drinks and left. Strolling back in the direction of my car, I kept looking around for Johnny, but he was nowhere in sight. When we passed a local wine shop, I was distracted by the display in the front window, large as life: aerosol spray cans of vintage wine dust from different years. Absolutely astonished, I asked Emily if she minded if we went inside. She didn't, so we did.

"Let me get this straight," I said to the chap behind the counter. "This is dust in a can, each one from a different year, correct?"

"You got it!"

"And, pray tell, what does one do with the dust?" I said, picking up a can and examining it.

Rolling his eyes, he informed me that one sprays it on one's bottles at home so they look aged. I told him that was all fine and dandy, but why the need for different years? "I would imagine all dust looks alike," I said.

He said it was because folks are vintage-obsessed.

"So if I blindfolded you and sprayed some 1999 and some 2003 wine dust on several different bottles, then removed the blindfold, you could tell me which was which?"

"Are you nuts? It's dust," the guy said, throwing his hands in the air like I was out of my mind.

He thought I was bonkers when he was the one selling dust in a can. Crazier yet was when he said he couldn't keep it in stock. *Only in California!*

As we stood there chatting, out of the corner of my eye, I could swear I caught Johnny Spezzo once again, spying through the shop's front window. He disappeared as soon as I took notice.

"Excuse me for a moment," I said, running out into the street. I looked left and right, but there was no sign of him. When I wandered back inside, scratching my head, both Emily and the shopkeeper looked at me strangely.

"What's wrong, Woody?" Emily said. "You've been acting so weird."

"Are you absolutely, 100 percent sure Johnny's in the big city?" I said, taking out a handkerchief and dabbing at the nervous moisture starting to form on my forehead.

"Seeing things?"

"Maybe!"

Soon, I left Emily, who had other things to do in Napa, got in my car, and headed to the estate in Carneros. I felt like I was being followed, but saw no one. At the estate, I looked for Amos, but couldn't find him. During my travels, though, I ran into McCall and inquired as to Horace's condition. As Emily had said, he was the same.

"Still no ransom note?" I said.

He simply shook his head.

"Mr. McCall," I said, "has it always been a man who's come out to examine your vault security system?"

He looked at me strangely. "That's a stupid question. Why?"

I told him I was just curious. He told me that only Joey Touchstone handled the vault.

Interesting, I thought. "So she never sent a guy out to do some adjustments in her place?"

He thought about it for a moment.

"No," he said bluntly. "Wait a minute. There may have been one time."

"When was this?" I said.

He thought about it for a moment.

"I believe it was the last time," he said, "a couple weeks before the dinner."

"Did you ask why he was there instead of Joey, sir?"

"She was sick or something," he said.

"Do you remember what the guy looked like?" I said.

"What the hell does it matter?"

"It's important, sir," I said, pushing the issue and leaning in.

"I do not," he said, getting agitated.

"So you remember that a man came out in place of Joey Touchstone, but you can't remember what he looked like?"

"Robins, you're starting to piss me off. What progress have you made?" he said, changing the subject.

Geez, he sure wasn't being very helpful, and I had to wonder if it was deliberate.

"I have a number of leads I'm working on," I said.

"And how close are you to a solution?"

I shifted from foot to foot, realizing that, no matter what I said, it probably would not be good enough. "Much closer, sir," was all I could muster.

"Remember, Robins, time is money. I want results," McCall said sternly, pounding his fist into his other open hand. He then walked away.

"Yes, Father," I muttered under my breath.

Just then, Ms. Svenson came by, leaving a track of mud behind her. It was strange—it hadn't rained for days. When I asked for Amos's where-abouts, she told me he was running some errands for her, but he would be off work at 5 p.m. She also told me the name of a bar just outside Ruther-ford he liked to frequent after work, called the Devil's Lair. How she knew this, I couldn't say, but I figured this would be a prime opportunity to tail him a bit and see what I could come up with, if anything.

The name of the bar sure didn't make it sound like a funhouse. It con-jured up images of bikers, roughhouses, and other unsavory characters. It seemed to fit.

If I was going to tail him, I couldn't use the 'Vette. My bright, canary yellow wheels would stand out like a sore thumb—and besides, he knew what I was driving. He also knew me. If I had to go into the bar, I'd need a disguise of some sort.

At about half past four, I donned a pair of bell-bottom jeans with cowboy boots, a black T-shirt, a leather vest, a wig, and aviator sunglasses. A costume shop had provided the getup. My wheels were rented—a black, four-door Chevy.

I hid outside the estate grounds up a secluded driveway and waited for Amos to return to the estate and leave again in his Hummer. At 5:10 p.m., the gates opened, and out drove Amos, but he wasn't in the car I thought he'd be in. He was behind the wheel of the Volkswagen Karmann Ghia. I was shocked. A guy his size behind the wheel of this small, sporty car looked, frankly, comical. How he could even comfortably fit in it was a mystery. Amos was certainly full of surprises.

He must have removed the muffler, too, because it sounded more thunderous than I'm sure it should have.

Keeping a good distance away, I followed him into Rutherford, to a dumpy little two-story house downtown. The neighborhood was kind of seedy and loud, with noisy kids playing all over the place. There were precious few trees on the street. All the houses were small and looked poorly constructed, mostly from aluminum siding. Not a single one showed any sign of house pride, like manicured lawns, trimmed hedges, potted plants, or nice paint jobs.

I parked up the street, on the other side, about one hundred yards away, behind another car—far enough away that I couldn't be seen, yet close enough so I could see Amos coming and going. Amos pulled into the driveway and went inside for a couple minutes. When he returned, he was accompanied by a woman in a hat. I was too far away to make out the details. I realized I needed to keep a pair of binoculars in the car for situations just like this. I reached for my tape recorder to record the idea, and when I again realized I didn't have it, I banged my hand down on the steering column, causing the horn to sound. Many of the kids close by stopped their frolicking and stared at me.

Way to go, Woody, I thought. *Give yourself away.* Amos stopped, apparently looking around to see where the noise was coming from, but didn't or couldn't find the source. *Thank God!*

When they got into his car and took off, I followed at a safe distance. They went across town to the east side, pulling up to an average-looking one-story stuccoed building. I parked up the road a good distance and watched. *This must be the place*, I thought. There were numerous cars and trucks, and even a few motorcycles parked out front. The folks coming and going didn't look so bad, and as Amos and the girl got out, I could see he was not in his work uniform, but dressed much nicer—dressy casual. I had to wonder why. The woman wore a pair of dark slacks, a light-colored blouse, a jacket, sunglasses, and, of course, the hat. I still couldn't make out who she was.

Damn it. I'm gonna have to go in there.

After pulling into their lot, I entered the place. It took a few moments for my eyes to adjust to the dim light. When they did, I was astonished. The place wasn't at all as I expected. It was actually quite nice. (Now I knew why Amos had dressed better!) There was a marble bar with fancy stools, numerous square tables with tablecloths, a banquet of cushioned booths, and a couple of antique pool tables. The walls were painted in light pastels and adorned with playful, surprisingly tasteful art, all depicting Lucifer and the underworld. Music played softly, and I recognized the piece: Tchaikovsky's *Waltz of the Flowers*. The folks inside were reasonably well dressed.

It was then I noticed that all eyes were on me.

I was so shocked at the bar's interior that I had completely forgotten what I looked like: a refugee from some sixties rock concert. *What was I thinking?* I just assumed the place would be a dive. I was petrified.

"Are you sure you're in the right place?" asked a nicely dressed waiter, looking me up and down.

I started to shake. Out of the corner of my eye, I spotted Amos and another guy just starting to shoot some pool at one of the tables. I didn't see his lady friend anywhere. I was already here, where I had to be, so I took a deep breath, got a grip on myself, and decided to see it through.

"Sure am," I said. "Just on my way to a costume party and thought I'd stop in for a quick drink."

My story seemed to appease the waiter, and he took off. Eventually, folks stopped staring at me, but I could hear them muttering and pointing off and on. Good thing Amos didn't take too much notice of me. I was extremely nervous, sweaty, and uncomfortable.

I walked up to the bar, not too far away from Amos and the other guy, and used a napkin to dry off my face. Then I ordered a Samuel Adams Boston Lager.

Turning once the drink arrived, I leaned against the bar, eyeing Amos and the other guy. Now I could see the details of Amos's dress. In a pair of khaki Dockers, a fern green shirt, and tennis shoes, he looked nothing like I'd expected. The other guy had on some black slacks and a polo shirt. They both looked respectable, but then I heard them talking about some item Amos had given him to try and sell.

Could they be talking about the wine? I thought.

The other guy said he had a buyer all lined up, but wasn't sure when the deal would take place. It occurred to me that, if Amos frequents a place like this, might he not be more appreciative of wine than he led me to believe? As I swung back to the bar to take a swig of my beer, I felt a tap on my shoulder.

"Hey, buddy, got a light?"

Turning around again, I just about had a conniption.

Standing before me, cigarette in hand, was Denise McCall. I hesitated for what seemed like a minute, but couldn't have been any more than five seconds.

"Sorry," I said, trying not to make eye contact.

What the hell was she doing here? Did she recognize me? If she blew my cover, I was cooked.

All of a sudden, Amos yelled over in our direction: "Hey, babe, did you see that shot?"

I looked around to see who he was talking to.

"Yeah, great!" Denise said.

Then it dawned on me: It was Denise. *She was with Amos?* Denise was the blonde I had seen getting into Amos's car, only I was too far away to make out who it was underneath the hat and sunglasses. I was flabbergasted. I didn't know what to do.

"Haven't seen you in here before," she said, looking me up and down. "Are you in a rock band?" She didn't seem to recognize me.

Amos, finishing up with the other guy, was now looking my way, and he didn't seem very happy.

"On my way to a costume party," I said. "Just passin' through!"

Oh my God, he was coming over. He stopped in front of me, drink in hand, put his other arm around Denise, and glared. My heart was in my mouth, and with the wig on, I was sweating bullets. I was incredibly scared—but not so much that I didn't notice his drink was a glass of red wine.

"Wanna shoot some pool?" Amos said, eyeballing me from stem to stern.

What to say?

"Thanks, but I'm outta here as soon as this beer is gone," I said, taking another swig.

The big guy just stood there, continuing to look me up and down. For a fraction of a second, I thought he recognized me. Time stood still.

Then he moved on, asking someone else if they wanted to play. *Thank God!*

I was done. This was too close for comfort. I downed the rest of my beer and left.

Once outside, I breathed a sigh of relief. My head was spinning.

Denise and Amos were in some sort of relationship. No wonder she found him "quite helpful." "Folks around here aren't all they appear to be" indeed!

Back in the car, I whipped off the wig. My hair beneath was soaked. As I sat there for several minutes, letting my heartbeat slow to normal, I went over in my mind what had just happened. I realized now how Amos had known the reason I would be asking questions. McCall hadn't mentioned to Amos why at all. Denise probably told him, and he stupidly said the boss did. That's probably also how he knew Emily didn't like him.

Was Amos involved in the theft or not? The two guys' conversation leaned in that direction, but just as it seemed they might divulge something incriminating, Denise stepped in and foiled it.

Boy, was Amos a chameleon, though. Though he seemed like a thug, he liked classical music, hung out at swank upscale bars, drove a nice sports car, and was even involved with a woman of money. And you could bet McCall didn't know about his daughter's involvement with the guy.

Earlier, I had almost dismissed Amos as a suspect, figuring most folks were hard on him just because of his looks. However, having discovered him drinking wine when he said he didn't, spotted the wine corks in his ashtray in the garage and, most importantly, overheard him in the bar talking about selling something, I was starting to rethink him. And if so, was Denise a part of the theft?

Thinking back on what I had just done, I questioned whether I was stupid, insane, or a little of both. Needless to say, it scared the bejesus out of me.

CHAPTER 17

B ack home in San Francisco, there were a few messages on my machine, one from Sadie asking how I was doing, and the other from Julia wanting to know if we were still on for dinner the next night. I called Sadie back first. I told her I still felt bad about the situation with Julia. When I mentioned that she was supposed to come over for dinner the next night and I was contemplating canceling, she advised me not to.

"I don't want to tell you what to do, Woody, but don't close that door unless you're ready to walk away," said Sadie. "We can't be absolutely sure the guy she was lunching with was a romantic interlude. And if you confront her, you might just push her into the arms of another man. If you have any hope of salvaging the situation, I'd say go through with dinner and do your best to pretend like nothing happened. Remember, she still loves you."

Good advice, I thought.

After we hung up, I called Julia. Getting her machine, I left a message letting her know we were still on for dinner at 6 p.m. Since I didn't have my tape recorder, I made a few notes about my earlier discoveries, this time on the computer so I could read them. After a final call to McCall to ask for the name and contact info of Amos's last employer, I took a quick shower and went off to bed. It had been quite a day.

The next morning, I called Amos's previous employer, a Mr. Spalding, pretending to be a prospective new employer looking for a reference. I inquired about his work habits, his ability as a mechanic and driver, his manner, his punctuality, his compatibility with other employees, and especially his trustworthiness. Mr. Spalding had only good things to say, but that didn't change his possible involvement in the wine theft.

After that, I prepared to go to the Gull—for work this time. Once a month, after the Gull has purchased the new wines I've suggested, I go in and conduct a tasting with the staff, talking about matching wines to food. Peter, one of the owners, says that since I started doing this, wine sales have skyrocketed.

After the session, I grabbed a quick bite there and headed home. I spent some time cleaning the house and preparing for dinner with Julia. At 5:55 p.m., I heard a knock at the front door. I opened it, and there Julia stood, holding a string-wrapped cardboard box with a peekaboo plastic window, and another small gift-wrapped package. She looked fantastic in a low-cut, aquamarine tank top, a pair of tight white jeans, and heeled white sandals. Under the circumstances, the sight of her made me feel weepy, but I fought it off.

She plastered herself against me and delivered a warm, sensual kiss.

"Hello, lover," she said. "I missed you." She seemed in a great mood. Stepping back, she examined me. "Honestly, Woody, where do you shop for clothes—Sally's from fifty years ago?"

I wasn't sure what she was talking about. I thought I looked great in a pair of baggy pin-striped triple-pleated black pants with cuffs, a pair of dark suspenders, and black and white bucks. The only variation on the theme was a bright red T-shirt that read, "Shaken, not stirred!"

"What's this?" I said, taking the box and gift-wrapped package from her.

"Dessert—chocolate cherry cheesecake!"

"Thanks, but not what I want for dessert," I said with a wink, trying my darndest to act as if nothing was wrong.

"Later, baby, later," Julia said.

"And the package?"

"A small gift," she said. "Go ahead and open it."

Placing the dessert down on the hall table, I ripped open the gift. It was a silver corkscrew with my name engraved on it. I was shocked.

"Thanks, hon," I said, giving her a kiss. "What's the occasion?"

"No occasion! Can't a gal simply give her guy a gift?" she said, brushing past me into the living room. "So how about a glass of wine?"

The fact that she was so affectionate, sweet, and generous made me feel all the worse, but I didn't show it. Going to the fridge, I uncorked an Aveleda Vinho Verde from Portugal, and poured a couple glasses. I love this stuff in the warm weather—it's fresh, lively, extremely crisp, and very low in alcohol. Plus it's a great starter, especially if you're planning on moving into other wines afterward.

We stepped out into the yard and sat on the wicker couch under the overhang.

"Can we eat out here tonight? It's such a lovely evening," she said.

"That's the plan."

After an hour of food, wine, superficial chat, and a few laughs, we went into the house and sat on the couch. So far, we were having a surprisingly wonderful evening. I asked what she had been up to.

"I'm continuing with my yoga classes, and just the other day bought some paint to redo that antique end table of mine. You know the one. And you remember my friend Louise who just had a baby? Well, I'm planning a shower for her. I've spent the last couple days driving around to caterers and printers for invitations trying to pull it together."

"How's the transmission in the car holding up?" I said, knowing she had been having trouble with it.

"The mechanic says it'll have to be replaced. That's a lot of money, so I'll probably start shopping around for a new car."

"And perhaps a new boyfriend," I muttered under my breath.

"I'm sorry. Did you say something?" she said, staring at me with those big, beautiful eyes.

"No—nothing," I said, remembering Sadie's advice.

She continued on: "Remember Lyn and John, that couple we doubled with about a month ago?"

I nodded.

"They're breaking up. They've been together for five years! That's a long time." She shrugged. "She said she just decided to move on."

"Just like you," I muttered to myself.

"Woody, what's with you tonight? You're acting so weird."

Although Sadie had advised against it, I couldn't help myself. It was eating me up inside, so I blurted it out: "Are you seeing someone else?"

She got a shocked look on her face and just about choked on her wine.

"Whatever gave you that idea?" she said, completely flummoxed.

"Word has it that you were out lunching with some guy the other day."

I expected her to look guilty, but she didn't.

"How do you know that?" she said, starting to get slightly upset. "Have you been spying on me?"

I ignored her question. "And you were getting quite cozy, holding hands."

Now her look of shock turned to anger as her face got flushed.

"If you're implying that I'm playing around on you, then you're quite mistaken," she said, turning away from me. "I would never do that to you."

"Then who was he?"

She turned back to me, took a deep breath, and in a soft, controlled voice, said, "It was an old friend I used to work with and happened to run into. He was down in the dumps, so we had lunch together. I thought I could cheer him up. That was it."

"What's his name?"

"Mark Nelson," she said.

"Do you have feelings for him?"

"What is this, an interrogation?" she said, standing up and walking around.

"Why were you holding hands?"

"He had just gone through a major breakup! He needed comforting."

"That doesn't explain why you were holding hands," I said.

"I was consoling him. He was in terrible shape. And I shouldn't have to explain myself to you like this," she said, crossing her arms and turning her back to me. "Don't you trust me?"

"I'm not sure," I said, hanging my head.

"Well, that's just great, Woody," she said, pacing around the room. "I've never ever given you *any* reason to mistrust me. That really hurts."

"So you're not interested in this guy?" I said.

No answer.

I repeated the question.

Still no answer. Julia just stood there with her back toward me.

"So?" I said.

She turned back toward me with tears in her eyes.

"He's gay, Woody."

"Excuse me?" I said, shaking my head as if coming out of a dream.

"Mark is gay."

I stood there with my jaw wide open. "But you never said—!"

"Why should I have to? You don't trust me—that's the crux of it. Maybe that's why you're having such a hard time deciding whether to live with me."

Shaking my head, I fumbled for some appropriate words to correct my stupidity, but came up empty.

"I'm so sorry, Julia. I don't know what came over me. Please, please forgive me," I said, trying to take her in my arms. But she would have none of it.

"I think I should go," she said sternly, stepping back and grabbing her bag.

"Please don't," I said, tears starting to fill my eyes. "Please don't go."

I couldn't blame her in the least for wanting to leave. Here I was, accusing her of fooling around on me (with a gay guy no less), implying I didn't trust her. And why? She had always been totally faithful to me. I felt so terrible, and guilty, too—guilty, because deep down, I felt stirrings for Emily, and was actually excited by the thought of her feeling likewise.

Christ, Julia even bought me a gift! What a schmuck I was!

I sat down on the couch, hung my head, and started crying. I sobbed for what seemed like an eternity, but couldn't have been any longer than thirty seconds, until Julia came over to me. Sitting down next to me on the couch, she took me in her arms. This time, when she spoke, her voice was tender.

"Look, Woody, I don't exactly know what's going on in your head or why you don't seem to trust me, but that's not a good basis for a relationship. You know how I feel about you," she said. "I love you dearly, but if you don't trust me, then there's no point of us even seeing each other, let alone living together."

"I do trust you, Julia, and I love you. I don't know what's wrong with me," I said, tears streaming down my face.

She said nothing, and just continued to hold me for a while. It felt good in her arms—safe and secure. I knew she was right.

After several minutes of closeness, we at last unlocked. I got up and poured her more wine, assuming she wasn't going to leave. We continued to sit quietly on the couch in silence. Trying to pull myself and her out of this funk, I changed the subject, asking how work was going. They were going to be doing some renovations at her office, she said, and it would be a nightmare for months. The Emporium had also registered her in a marketing course that they would be paying for.

Since we were on the subject of work, I asked Julia if anyone had approached the Emporium about the wine, briefly filling her in on some of the details about the missing vintage.

"Not a soul," she said.

"You folks usually purchase product through agents, don't you?" I said.

"Most of the time," she said. "Occasionally, we'll buy from an auction house, or directly from a producer, cutting out the middleman. Agents aren't fond of that approach."

I asked if they ever bought from individuals or private collectors. She said she never recalled them doing that. The problem was not knowing the provenance of the wine—how it was stored and its authenticity.

"But it is possible?"

"I guess," she said.

"Dessert?"

"I'm stuffed," Julia said. But she suggested playing pool—I suppose in an attempt to lighten up the mood. I wasn't sure I wanted to do anything, the way I was feeling, but I agreed.

Getting up from the couch, I poured a couple of Spanish brandies from a great bottle that Miguel Torres himself produced and gave me personally. Down in the rec room, I turned on the radio and found an oldies station—great music for pool, and great for taking my mind off our relationship woes.

But after shooting a couple games—which, by the way, I lost—we turned in. I was actually surprised she wanted to stay the night after my behavior. But if you must know, there was no hanky-panky.

I was shocked out of my sleep by the ringing phone. *Who the hell is calling at this hour?* I thought, not really sure what hour it was. I keep my bedroom so dark you can't really tell what's going on outside.

Picking up the phone, I looked over at Julia, who was stirring but still asleep. The bedside clock said 10:30 a.m. We really must have conked out.

"Mr. Robins, it's Mr. Philips."

"Sorry, who?" I was still half-asleep.

"Joe Philips. Bonham & Butterfields Auction House on San Bruno Avenue," he said, sounding frantic.

It was the last of the three auction houses I had visited. Mr. Philips was the wine expert there. He was a well-dressed guy about sixty-five years of age, with gray hair and a pair of granny glasses that sat precariously on the end of his beezer.

"Ah, Mr. Philips. What's up?" I said, trying to shake the cobwebs.

He said he needed to see me immediately.

"That wine you asked me about? I've just been approached with it. It's incredible."

He sounded extremely upset.

"You need to come . . ."

"Hello? Hello? Mr. Philips, are you there?" I said.

The silence at the other end of the line was shattering. I suddenly had a very bad feeling.

CHAPTER 18

I rang the auction house buzzer, but there was no response. I saw no sign of Philips through the window. Finally, I tried the door, and much to my surprise, it swung open.

"Mr. Philips, are you here?" I said, entering cautiously. "It's Woody Robins."

No answer. Slowly, I walked up to the counter.

"Mr. Philips, it's Woody Robins. Are you here?"

Still no answer!

As I neared the counter, I saw a pair of legs stretched out on the floor. I came around the side of the counter, and there he was, lying on his back in a pool of blood, eyes open, staring coldly at the ceiling. There was a huge gash in his right temple. A blood-covered antique bung mallet lay next to him.

"Oh my God!" I yelled, panicking and staggering back, almost falling over myself. It was horrible. His blank, lifeless eyes gave me the willies. I danced from side to side with nervous hysteria, trying to figure out what to do. I started to hyperventilate.

Then I remembered what folks often did on TV or in the movies when confronted with this situation. They checked the body for a pulse. So I raced to his side and started to put my fingers on his neck, but pulled back. Where on his neck was I supposed to feel? I didn't know. I found a spot off to one side and touched. I couldn't feel anything, but he was still warm. But when I actually realized I was touching a stiff, I freaked out and jumped back.

I began to walk in circles, trying to decide what to do next. I wondered if whoever did this was still around. That concept scared the crap out of me, so I hustled my butt outside pronto. Pulling out my cell phone,

I dialed Detective George Gold.

After I gave my statement, I sat in my car for a while, completely stunned. I had seen dead bodies before in real life, but only at viewings in funeral parlors where the person was made up like a kabuki.

During the drive back home, I tried to piece together what might have happened. The thief must have been pretty desperate to approach an auction house directly. As I said before, such an action would most certainly give away the crime. Even when I visited these houses in the first place, it was a complete long shot, and I really didn't expect anything to come of it. Go figure. But whether Philips had agreed or refused to find a buyer, or even if he'd offered to buy it himself for sale through auction, there was no reason for murder. I didn't get it.

I was in shock—so much so that, before I knew it, I was pulling into my driveway in North Beach next to Julia's Camaro. The smell of freshly brewed coffee greeted me as I walked in. Julia made me a cup as I filled her in on what had happened.

Later, Georgey came by to chat, and I told him the entire story, from the time I met with Professor Pendry at UC Davis until the moment I called him from the auction house. I also filled him in on all my discoveries, at least the ones I could remember without the help of my stupid tape recorder.

Georgey told me the murder had indeed been committed with the bung mallet. Bung mallets were used one hundred years ago to bang the bung into the bunghole of wine barrels after they were topped up. He said it would not have rendered Philips immediately unconscious, so his death had more than likely been excruciatingly painful.

I didn't need to hear more.

McCall had wanted this investigation extremely low-key, but now, it seemed destined for the spotlight.

Hours later, still reeling from my discovery, I finally listened to a message on my office machine. It was from McCall, saying he was having a soiree for friends, family, and business associates at his house the following Tuesday at 7 p.m. In his inimitable style, he ordered me to come, as it would be a good opportunity to view folks and see if anything related to the theft came to light.

As much as I didn't like to be ordered around, it actually was a good idea. It would also allow me the opportunity to do a little uninterrupted snooping around the house, maybe in Lambeck and Svenson's rooms without them standing over me. I never did get a good look-see the first time.

I rang Charlie to see if he was available. It didn't take him two seconds to say yes. I figured I'd better tell him about the murder and ask him if he still wanted to go. When I did, there was a long silence.

"Free grub, free booze, and plenty of available rich chicks?" he said. "I'm in." I provided him with the address and directions.

"Remember, Sherlock, this is an upscale business engagement, not a frat party," I said. "You can schmooze, but keep your eyes and ears open for anything that might be helpful to the case. You understand?"

"I dig, boss!" he said. "Maybe I'll wear that blue tuxedo my uncle laid on me."

"You most certainly will not," I said.

"Oh, please," said Charlie. "What about you and your flashy duds?"

"Oh, fine, wear what you want!" I still felt way too frazzled about the murder to argue with him.

I then placed the call I dreaded. Dialing McCall, I asked him first if my assistant could accompany me to the soiree. When he agreed, I said we would be there. Then I told him about the murder—better me than the police. He immediately wanted to cancel the affair, but I advised him not to. His idea of observing the attendees did indeed make a lot of sense.

Tuesday rolled around quickly, and the image of poor Mr. Philips lying there in that pool of blood still haunted me.

It was about half past five when I headed up to Carneros and the estate. It wouldn't hurt to get there a bit early and check things out before folks arrived.

When I got to the gate at about 6:40, though, it was already open, and folks were coming and going freely. Pulling around to the front of the house, I found numerous vehicles parked. Service people were every-where. The front door was open, so I walked in.

Florists were busily arranging bouquets, and I saw two long buffet tables groaning with food, one indoors in the dining room and the other out by the pool. Men were putting the finishing touches on the lighting strung around the patio, and some hired wait staff were hustling about with china and cutlery. Meandering about inside the house, I noticed two separate bars stocked and ready to go. Out by the pool, another bar was about to open shop, and a small musical ensemble, off to one side, started to play. *Boy, when the rich throw a party, they mean business,* I thought.

Strolling into the kitchen, I found Roberto orchestrating food prep like a conductor. We saluted each other, and I moved on. In the hallway just outside the living room, I ran into Ms. Svenson.

"Lots of traffic here," I said.

"Oh, Mr. Robins, yes. I'm going crazy. So many fires to put out! My, don't you look sharp," she said, giving me a quick up and down.

I thanked her for the compliment and asked where McCall was. I figured I should check in with him. She told me she had last seen him in the library, so I headed that way.

When I entered the library, I found the boss elegantly dressed in a black tuxedo. He was on the phone with somebody. Hanging up, he turned and saw me.

"Is everything okay?" I said.

Before he spoke, McCall gave me the once-over and shook his head. I don't know why. I was wearing a cream-colored, double-breasted wool dinner jacket with pencil-gray, triple-pleated, baggy slacks and a cranberry linen, collarless shirt, along with black suspenders. On my noggin was a three-inch, wide-brimmed, dark gray zoot suit hat with a white band.

"I've got to tell you, Robins, I'm very nervous about this whole affair since that murder," McCall said, picking up a whiskey he had been nursing. "The thought of possibly having that person in my house rattles me. I should have cancelled the damn thing."

"You'll be fine, sir. I have faith in you," I said, trying to put him at ease.

"Well, I'm glad someone does," he said, nervously taking another slug of his drink. "You keep a good eye out."

I assured him my assistant and I would be on it like hawks.

When I went back out, the place was already jumping. All the service people and workers were gone, with lots of well-dressed folks in their place. Couples were dancing out by the pool as the ensemble played some old standards. The buffet outside was jammed with all kinds of wonderful edibles: shrimp, lobster, oysters, salads, cold cuts, and breads, with a guy at one end carving prime rib.

I worked my way to one of the fully stocked bars to examine what was on tap. Off to one side, Mumm bubbly sat chilling in an ice bucket. I requested a glass.

As I took the flute from the barkeep, I heard, from behind, "Hey, sailor, buy a girl a drink?"

I turned around to find Emily in a sensational short, black, silk cocktail dress, with matching black stilettos.

"I'm sipping bubbly. Would you like some?" I said, taking her in.

I asked for another glass and gave it to her. Looking around, I asked where Johnny was. She told me he was on his way and would meet her shortly.

I was about to say something when she grabbed my hand and said, "Let's dance."

We put our glasses down and headed out onto the dance floor, joining the other couples tripping the light fantastic. We shuffled our tail feathers as the band played "Boogie Woogie Bugle Boy," but the next tune was a slow one, and she cuddled up close. She was warm and soft, and purred in my ear. She smelled amazing. Her perfume was making me crazy. It felt really, really good to be in her arms—so much so that I almost forgot about Julia, not to mention Emily's boyfriend, who would be showing up any moment.

Suddenly, reality kicked in, and I was hit instantly by a wave of guilt. Just as I was about to pull away and guide her off the dance floor, she whispered in my ear, "Oh Woody, if I didn't have a boyfriend . . ."

The words melted into my heart, and I instantly felt as if I was in a sort of dream.

All of a sudden, we were bumped. I turned around.

"Pardon me," I started to say, until I saw who it was. "Well, cut off my legs and call me Shorty. If it isn't Mr. Cuddle!"

"Woody, it's you," said Charlie. He was with a dark-haired cutie.

"No, it's Claudette Colbert in drag," I said, rolling my eyes.

"You look like a Chicago gangster," he said, examining me from head to toe.

As least I was recognizable. Charlie had worn the aforementioned blue tuxedo, along with a frilly shirt and a red bow tie. He looked like a fugitive from a 1960s prom night. He introduced Maria, about Emily's age with jet-black hair in a flip and big brown eyes. In a short, green taffeta cocktail dress, she was an interesting contrast to Charlie's blue delirium.

To Emily, I introduced Charlie as my assistant. The girls hugged, obviously knowing one another. The band suddenly burst into another up-tempo number.

"Oh, Charlie, I love this tune. Let's dance!" Maria squealed, taking him by the hand. "Good meeting you, Woody!" she cried as they gyrated away on the dance floor.

I guided Emily off the dance floor and we retrieved our drinks. Standing there, we sheepishly stared at each other, wondering what to say. It didn't take a Ph.D. to figure out the rest of that sentence that had trailed off on the dance floor.

"What's wrong?" Emily said, seeing the look on my face. "You look sad."

"Nothing," I said, taking a sip of my drink.

I changed the subject and asked who Maria was. It turned out she was Johnny Spezzo's sister. My buddy-cum-assistant Charlie had hooked up with just the right dame. Who knew what Charlie might pick up from her about her brother's possible involvement in the theft? It would probably be a good idea to inform Charlie at some point who she was so he could pay extra attention to anything she might say.

As Emily and I strolled around, she pointed out certain people.

"See that stout, elderly man over there by the other bar—the one in the brown suit with the young woman on his arm?" she said.

"You mean the pop tart?"

She looked at me funny, then continued, "That's Father's accountant, Roland Digmore. And that bleach-blonde, middle-aged woman over there, wearing that little chiffon number that's way too short for her?" She pointed toward the buffet table. "Linda Grable, husband of the late Winston Grable, oil tycoon! She's worth a bundle."

She continued to point out people, including a little man in a gray suit who looked as if he had escaped from Fantasy Island. He was Paulo Vicente, a jockey. And just as she was about to comment on someone else, Johnny showed up.

"Thanks for taking care of my lady, Woody," Johnny said, giving Emily a hug and a peck on the cheek.

I have to admit, there was a very small part of me deep inside that wished Johnny had not shown up. *I'm a terrible person*, I thought. Then it dawned on me that I hadn't yet seen Denise. I asked Emily where she was.

"She's somewhere," she said, clipped.

I wondered if I'd run into her with Amos.

Excusing myself, I wandered around solo, watching people interact. I eavesdropped on a few conversations, looking for any kind of hint or suggestion regarding the missing wine. At one point, I got into a conversation with a Dr. Linkletter, a used-parts salesman for humans. As he was bending my ear, I spotted Charlie going inside alone. Excusing myself, I caught up with him.

"Hey, Casanova, a word, please!" I said.

"Not now, man! I gotta water my shilelee," Charlie said, anxious to get away.

"Listen," I whispered. "Maria is the sister of one of the suspects. She might give something away. Whatever you do, don't mention what we're all about, okay?"

"What *who's* all about?" he said, looking confused.

I had to take a deep breath.

"The Ghost and Mrs. Muir!" I said. "Who the hell do you think? You and I!"

"After all these years, dude, you still don't know when I'm yankin' your chain."

I continued to tell him that, if she asked how we came to be at this party, he should make something up. He said he was way ahead of me — he'd already told her we were doing some consulting for McCall.

It wasn't the greatest line, but I supposed it would do.

"Remember, eyes and ears open!" I hissed as Charlie ran off to the can.

As I continued to stroll about, I wasn't surprised to run into numerous winery owners and winemakers. They probably bought grapes from McCall. When they asked why I was there, I simply used the same line Charlie had suggested. This seemed to appease them, and they carried on. I proceeded to walk around leisurely, looking for anything that might enlighten this case.

CHAPTER 19

The party was now in full swing. I looked around for both Lambeck and Svenson. I saw them running in and out of the house, carrying this and cleaning up that. They were busier than a mongoose in a chicken coop. *Good*, I thought. *Now I can do some real snooping.* After all, they were the two people who had access to the entire dwelling on a regular basis, and of all the staff, they were the closest to McCall. I needed a better look at their rooms.

I went into the house and up to the second floor. It was quiet up there. Looking up and down the hall, I tried Lambeck's door. *Damn!* It was locked. I pulled out my wallet and retrieved one of my credit cards. I'd always seen folks use a credit card in the movies to jimmy open a lock by pushing it between the door and the frame, but had never tried it myself. I played with it for a good two minutes, but nothing happened. Flipping the card over, I tried it again.

Suddenly, I heard a click. I turned the knob and the door opened. *Wow, I did it.* Going inside, I shut the door and locked it behind me.

I noted ornate framed paintings and a gilded mirror decorating the walls. The door to the small balcony was slightly ajar.

I quickly rummaged through the closet but found nothing of any significance. I wasn't even sure what I was looking for. I knew Lambeck was connected to the mob, but I suppose I was looking for something specific that would point to the theft. As I started to go through one of the drawers in the bureau, I heard someone at the door—then a key in the lock.

Holy crap, I thought, *I'm going to be caught!*

Closing the drawer, I looked around for a place to hide, deciding on the balcony. I stepped out and shimmied up to the side so I couldn't be seen. Looking down at the crowd below, I felt stupid. What if someone noticed me skulking up here? Fortunately for me, people were too busy to take notice or to care.

I heard Lambeck cursing in his New York accent about how sloppy people can be. Carefully peering into the room, I could see he had a huge wine stain on his shirt, which he proceeded to change. For one second there, he stopped and cocked his head, as if listening for something. I feared he might have heard me somehow. But he then continued on, and when done, he left and locked up.

I breathed a sigh of relief. *That was close*, I thought.

Stepping back into the room, I continued to go through the drawer. Leafing through some papers, there were numerous casino gambling receipts, and the names "Dentico" and "Cirillo" kept popping up. Whether they had any significance or not, I didn't know, but I pulled a piece of paper out of my jacket and jotted them down. I could hear some voices outside in the hallway again and decided it was time to get out of here. I waited patiently for the voices to fade and disappear and then, opening the door and peering out in both directions, locked up and left.

Next on my list was Svenson's room. It was locked as well. I tried the credit card thing again, but this time with no success. But maybe I could get in if I had something to actually fit into the keyhole. I found a bobby pin in the washroom of a nearby, unoccupied bedroom. Heading back to Ms. Svenson's room, I started working on the lock. But then, as an elderly couple came walking by, I had to pretend I was heading to the washroom.

As soon as they were gone, I worked the pin into the lock, hoping for some success. There was nothing at first, but I kept at it.

Then, bingo! It clicked, and in I went, locking the door behind me.

Again, I didn't know what I was looking for. I was just hoping for something that might point me in the right direction.

In Svenson's top dresser drawer, there was little of any significance—just more unframed photos, several of a newborn. *Probably a niece or nephew!* There was also a postcard sent from Los Angeles, which said, "It was nice having you around. Miss you. Love, Andrea." An older letter, dated almost twenty-four years ago, was from the Human Services Agency of San Francisco. It said, "Thanks." A couple of toiletry items, including an opened can of baby powder, topped off that drawer's contents.

In another drawer, I came across a folder that contained what appeared to be a love letter from an old beau. It simply read, "We'll be together soon." No signature! The folder also contained her legal documents. Although there was a Danish passport, there weren't any immigration papers. That seemed odd to me.

I looked around a bit more, but found nothing else, so I left.

I contemplated going into Denise's room, since she was so adamant about me not seeing it, but I wasn't sure where it was and didn't want to go trying all the other locked rooms. Besides, since I hadn't yet seen her, she might even be in there. I considered checking out Emily's room, but again, I didn't know which one it was. I even toyed with the idea of going through McCall's room, as he had completely and vigorously dismissed the idea when I first brought it up the day we met, but I gave it up for Lent. If I did search there, and somehow he got wind of it—or worse, actually caught me—he'd go snaky for sure and right off the deep end. Besides, all this sneaking about was making me extremely nervous. I was sweating under my clothes, and my heart was racing.

Once back downstairs with the other partiers, I breathed a sigh of relief. I wondered if I was cut out for all this breaking in and snooping. Grabbing another glass of bubbly from one of the bars, I strolled about, watching people and homing in on numerous conversations. I ran into Sam Spezzo and his wife Lucy and, later, Ralph Wader and his wife, Jane. I hadn't met Jane before. She was a nice-looking lady about Ralph's age and height, with dark red hair and horn-rimmed glasses.

As I was chatting with them, I spotted Denise scurrying off in the direction of the cottage. Excusing myself, I took off in pursuit. I had no idea where exactly she was going, but she was moving with such conviction that I felt compelled to follow. Maybe she was meeting up with Amos, and I could pick up something more from them regarding the wine. But I lost her somewhere along the path leading to the small stone bridge.

When I got closer, though, I heard some voices growing louder as I moved along. They were coming from some nearby bushes.

Focusing on the spot, crouching down and parting several large ferns, I discovered a small clearing where two people sat on a wrought-iron bench, cuddling, kissing, and quietly chatting.

"I missed you," Amos said.

"I missed you," said Denise.

"Did anybody see you coming this way?"

"I don't think so," Denise said, looking around.

They continued to canoodle. I watched them for several minutes before realizing I was going to learn nothing from this reconnaissance, so I returned to the crowd at the house. There, I saw no sign of my comrade in arms, Charlie. Maybe he got lucky.

By this point, the get-together was starting to break up, and I thought it best to find the boss and check in before heading home. I found him inside at one of the other bars. Before I approached, I noticed Ms. Svenson off to one side of the room, staring at him, again with that same look she had displayed at the dinner the first night. Very strange!

I went up to McCall and expressed my thanks for the invite. Then I left for my car.

There, I found an envelope stuck under my windshield wiper—and my right front tire slashed. *What the hell?!* I thought.

The computer-generated note simply read, "Back off or else!"

I looked around to see if anyone who might have planted it was lurking about. There were plenty of folks getting in their cars and driving off, but no one who looked suspicious. This case was getting weirder all the time, and I was getting scared. This second letter, and the accompanying destruction of private property, could mean only one thing, though: I must be getting closer.

After waiting well over an hour for roadside assistance to show up, I headed out.

Back home in my office, I searched the house again for my tape recorder but came up empty.

So instead, I noted on the computer what I had discovered in Lambeck's room. My thoughts once again turned to that mob-related fact that I swear I had noted in a recording. It was driving me nuts.

Sleep did not come easy that night. Too many things were rumbling around in my brain.

CHAPTER 20

The next day, I worked on a number of other projects. My computer consultant also came out and changed a few things on my website. He warned me about a wicked virus going around that could freeze my computer screen. I assumed it was the same one Johnny Spezzo had mentioned that first night at the estate when he fixed McCall's computer.

About mid-afternoon, I placed a call to Charlie to see if he had picked up anything of significance from Maria about Johnny's possible involvement in the theft. According to Charlie, the only thing she said was that Johnny had seemed very secretive about something recently. Maybe the secret was the stolen wine.

The rest of the day was spent doing some research for the new book, writing another column, and catching up on e-mail. Another sleepless night ensued.

Sitting back in my chair the next day, I thought of how disturbed I felt about this case. I was haunted by the image of Philips lying there dead, the threatening notes and the slashed tire scared the crap out of me, and the Mafia could be involved. On top of that, my aunt was in pain, and my love life seemed doomed for the crapper.

It didn't get any better, either. Just before noon, when I returned from having my slashed tire repaired, there was a message on my office machine. It was from McCall.

There had been a car accident. Johnny Spezzo was dead.

When I called the estate, Ms. Svenson, who answered the phone, was so distraught she couldn't talk. McCall took the phone from her and explained what had happened. Johnny had been driving home to San Francisco a few hours earlier, having stayed over after the party. He lost control of his car and ran into a tree. He died instantly.

"Emily must be devastated," I said.

"She's beside herself."

I asked when the funeral was, and was told it was tomorrow morning.

At about 8:45 a.m. the next day, I headed out to midtown for Johnny Spezzo's funeral at St. Patrick Catholic Church. Most of the people there were older. I assumed they had come out of respect for Johnny's father, Sam.

All the McCalls were there.

Patricia, who had not attended the party a few days earlier, looked completely wrung out, teary, and gaunt. I was sure Horace's condition was still taking its toll on her. Emily was a write-off, sobbing constantly. I gave her a hug. It was strange to see Denise in a dress, but she looked fantastic. The idea of her and Amos still muddled my thoughts. She was sad but didn't cry. The boss just nodded in my direction.

I approached the Spezzos and offered my condolences. Lucy had to be supported and consoled by Sam and Maria every second. I nodded at the Waders and shook my head. Rossi hung his head, looking sad. Lambeck was there, and I watched him carefully to see his reaction. He didn't seem to show any emotion whatsoever, and that bothered me. Ms. Svenson, on the other hand, was extremely broken up. That was odd, too. She must have felt awfully close to Johnny, since he was around so much.

It was a sad affair.

I was not surprised to see Joey Touchstone. I attempted to catch up with her when the service ended. She tried to avoid me, but eventually, I managed to confront her.

"Why didn't you return my phone calls?" I said.

"I was extremely busy," she said, in a nonchalant way. "Besides, I have nothing else to say to you."

"I guess I'll have to call the police," I said, taking out my cell phone, threatening to dial just as I did when I first met her.

"Go ahead," she said. "I don't give a damn."

She really didn't seem to care this time. It would only be a matter of time until the police came to her anyway, in their investigation of Philips's murder, so I backed off.

Sitting in my office afterwards, I thought about my next move. Just because Johnny Spezzo was out of the picture didn't mean he wasn't involved with the theft. Touchstone's attitude didn't help their case.

I checked in with my aunt to see how she was doing. She didn't say, but I could tell by her voice that she was in a lot of pain, and it was getting worse. She wanted to know how my evening with Julia had gone. I relayed what had happened.

"Well, doesn't that just take the cake?" she said, laughing. "A gay guy, eh? Just goes to show that everything isn't always as it seems."

"It's not a laughing matter, Aunt Sadie," I said, starting to get upset. "Now she thinks I don't trust her."

"Well, do you?"

"I guess so, but she's convinced I don't. She says lack of trust is no basis for a relationship—let alone living together," I said. "Even if love is there!"

"The lady does have a point, my boy," said Sadie. "So where do you two stand?"

"In limbo," I said. "I don't think we're broken up, but we're not exactly moving forward, either. What am I going to do?"

"Get over yourself and ask her to move in," she said, quite bluntly. "You're skating on mighty thin ice here, and if you don't make a decision soon, it will be too late."

I didn't want to hear that, but knew it was true.

There was silence for a minute before she spoke again. She asked how work was going.

"It's going fine," I said.

"Yeah? Well, something in your voice says otherwise. You sound frustrated."

"No, I'm fine," I said.

"Spill it," she said.

"Really, I'm fine."

"Woody!" she said.

"All right!" I said, exasperated. I never could hide anything from Sadie. "It's going very slowly, and the guy I'm working for is infuriating," I said.

"And how's that?"

I usually don't go into detail about stuff I'm working on, with my aunt or anyone else, because I believe it's unethical. However, right now, I felt really lonely, abandoned, and down in the dumps, and I knew she would understand about McCall.

"He's not your father," Sadie said. "Keep that in perspective."

"I know, I know. But it's hard. I react emotionally."

"Just keep reminding yourself: He's *not* my father."

Whether talking to Sadie a bit about McCall was helpful or not, it felt good to confide in someone—so much so that I made the mistake of telling her more about the case than I had actually planned on. I told her of the threatening letters and the slashing of my tire, Horace Botner's beating, Philips's murder, and Johnny Spezzo's demise. Of course, Sadie reacted.

"Christ, Woody, take yourself off this case immediately! I don't want to be receiving a call someday saying . . ." She couldn't finish the sentence, and silence prevailed for the next few moments until she finally spoke again.

"Be bloody careful in this case until it's over, Woody. Watch your back constantly. Do you understand me?"

"Absolutely," was all I could say. She really did care about me.

When I hung up, I went back to work. I found the piece of paper on which I had jotted the two names I found among casino gambling receipts in Lambeck's dresser drawer. I did a Google search on them.

Holy Hannah! Both guys were part of the Genovese family of New York. Lawrence "Little Larry" Dentico and Dominick "Quiet Dom" Cirillo were henchmen for Mario Gigante, brother of Vincent "Chin" Gigante, who used to be the head honcho of the whole crime family. When I'd found out Lambeck was connected to the mob, I hadn't guessed it would run this deep. As to whether they had somehow played into the theft, it was still questionable, but this didn't bode well.

Suddenly, my cell rang. It was Georgey. He had gotten the lab results back from the murder. He talked me into picking up a large pizza and six-pack and coming to his place to talk things over.

Georgey lives on the top floor of a three-story brownstone walk-up in the Haight-Ashbury part of town. The area is most famous for its 1960s hippy culture. I made the right turn onto his street and pulled around to the visitor parking area in the back of his building. A guy was coming out the front door of Georgey's building, so he didn't have to buzz me in.

Up on the third floor, Georgey let me into his one-bedroom pad. Large windows looked eastward toward the bay. Although Georgey was sloppy in his dress, his place was immaculate. Modern chic furnishings combined color, metal, and fabric into a sharp, bright décor. Framed posters of comic book superheroes and cartoon characters adorned the walls, and a rich, chocolate-brown Berber carpet lay underfoot. The *Star Wars* soundtrack was playing on the stereo, and Georgey was air-conducting the orchestra.

I set the pizza and beer down on the coffee table right next to a plastic-covered *Green Lantern* comic and hit the can. When I came out, Georgey was already into the food and suds. Sitting down, I cracked a beer and grabbed a pizza slice. When I took a swig and put the can down on the coffee table, I got myself into trouble.

"For God's sakes, man, use a coaster!" Georgey said, tossing me one and taking one of the napkins I'd brought to dry the wet spot my beer can had made.

"Yes, Mother!"

"Great pie, though! You remembered to get the hot peppers. Whew, they got a real bite in the back end," he said, delivering a burp so loud they probably heard it on Telegraph Hill.

"So what's up with the lab report?" I said.

Pulling out a notebook from his jacket pocket, Georgey started rambling off Philips's specs.

"Age: sixty-five. Married with two grown kids. One month away from retire—"

"Whoa, Georgey, get to the point please," I said.

"Sorry! Time of death was approximately 10:30 a.m."

"That's twenty-five minutes before I even arrived," I said. *He must have been hit while I was on the phone with him,* I thought. *That's why his voice trailed off.* "Did they find any prints on the murder weapon?"

"They did," he said, "but they were so badly smudged they couldn't properly ID them."

"What about the surveillance camera? Those places always have them."

"It wasn't working."

Georgey put his notebook down and took another piece of pizza from the box. I did likewise. Neither of us said anything for a few minutes. The detective finally broke the silence.

"There didn't appear to be much of a struggle," he said. "Looked like he wasn't expecting it. The coroner said that, from the angle of the blow, it more than likely was administered by a southpaw."

We continued our munching and, within minutes, the pie was gone.

"Is there anything else?" I said, wiping my face with a napkin.

"Just one thing," said Georgey. "A lone, dark brown hair was found on the body."

"So a left-handed, brown-haired person was the murderer? Just look at all the possible culprits: employees, customers, my suspects—geez, even his wife! Isolate the southpaws and see who was a brunette," I said.

"Thanks for telling me how to do my job," Georgey said. Turns out it wasn't quite that simple. "Some people are ambidextrous," he said, "and not all sport their natural hair color." Nonetheless, he would be pulling Philips's employee and customer records, as well as investigating my suspects very carefully.

"When you assemble the list of employees and customers, just give it to me and I'll check them out," I said.

"No can do. This is a murder investigation, and you're not a cop."

As we sat there, digesting and finishing off the beers, Georgey's phone rang. "Gold here," he said.

He listened very carefully for a few minutes. "Okay, I'm on my way," he said. He hung up and turned to me. "Look, kiddo, gotta run. Thanks for the feed!"

"No problem, buddy," I said.

We both left together. He said he would be in touch.

CHAPTER 21

I needed to go back out to the estate and do a little more investigating. During the drive, it crossed my mind that, if Johnny Spezzo was somehow involved, and the Mafia too, perhaps his death wasn't exactly an accident.

I also went over my theories of the theft. Theory one: Johnny and Touchstone sabotaged the security system to steal the wine. Emily may or may not have been involved. Theory two: Perhaps Lambeck, along with his mob buddies, lifted it. Theory three: Maybe Amos did it and was trying to sell it. If so, was Denise involved? The final theory was that Horace somehow stole the wine to pay off gambling debts. There was evidence to back all four ideas. And what of the murder? If Horace was in the hospital in a coma when it went down, he couldn't possibly be the murderer.

When I arrived at the estate, I strolled around the main house, looking at its structure for something that might enlighten me as to how the wine got out. Who did it was key, but *how* was the next biggest question: Up to this point, I hadn't spent much time considering that aspect. Did the thief simply go through the front or back door, or was there some sort of a secret entrance?

An exhaustive search of the house's perimeter yielded nothing, so I rang the doorbell. Lambeck greeted me. I was surprised. It was getting harder to look him in the face and play along with his charade, but I did. Until I got what I was looking for, the show must go on.

When I asked where Ms. Svenson was, I was informed she was so upset that she was taking the day off. I found McCall in his study reading the newspaper.

"So, what have you got for me, Robins?" the boss said briskly.

"How's Emily holding up?"

"Not well," he said.

I asked him once again about a ransom note. There was none. But when I inquired as to whether he had blueprints of the house, it set him off.

"Blueprints? What, are you an architect now?" said McCall. "Robins, you're starting to get under my skin."

I explained what I was looking for. I could tell by the expression on his face that he thought the idea of a secret entrance was nuts, but he did finally concede that Wader had a copy in his office in San Francisco.

"By the way," I said, "is Ms. Svenson a legal immigrant?"

"Why on God's earth does that matter?" said McCall. "She's been in America so long. You really ask the stupidest questions, Robins."

I ignored McCall's remark and let him go back to his paper. Back out at my car, I was amazed to find the hood open and Dan Amos tinkering. He was whistling Prokofiev's *Peter and the Wolf*.

"What are you doing?" I said, peering into the open hood.

"I thought I'd do that valve adjustment for you."

I thanked him and told him I appreciated it. When he needed another tool, he went into the garage and I followed. This time, I noticed some candles and a lantern on one of the shelves. Maybe I had seen them the first time I examined the garage, but they hadn't struck me as important at the time. Since following Amos and linking him more closely to the potential theft, they seemed to take on more significance, so I asked about them.

"They're for blackouts," he said, grabbing a big monkey wrench.

"Blackouts?"

Amos explained that they occasionally had blackouts, and he needed some source of light when it happened, especially at night. I asked when the last one was.

"About a month ago," he said. When I asked for an exact date, he couldn't remember. He did say it was the evening, though.

He continued to work on my car. Finishing up, he grabbed his tools and went back into the garage. As he left, I asked him something.

"Do you have a corkscrew, Mr. Amos?"

He turned and gave me a look that could kill.

"What the hell does that mean?" he said.

God, he's a menacing-looking thing. I took two steps backwards.

"Nothing," I said, quickly getting into my car.

Maybe I was being paranoid here, but did he really adjust the valve?

After all, I had been threatened twice recently and had my tire slashed. Just to ease my mind, before getting on the highway back to San Francisco, I stopped at the nearest gas station in Carneros to have a mechanic give my car a quick once-over. I told him I'd heard a funny rattle. Fortunately, all was fine.

On the drive back, I contemplated the candles, the lantern, and the blackouts. Nobody had mentioned blackouts before. It seemed a good possibility that the theft of the wine could have been done during a blackout. It would certainly make the job easier. I pulled over for a minute, scribbled the idea down on a piece of paper, and stuck it in my briefcase before continuing on.

Suddenly, my cell rang. It was Julia. I was surprised to hear from her.

"Are you all right?" I said, hoping nothing was wrong. Our last get-together had turned into quite a heavy affair.

"I'm fine," she said. "Just called to let you know that the Emporium was approached late yesterday about buying a 1784 red Burgundy."

"Who took the call?"

"I did," she said.

"Was the caller a man or woman?"

"I really couldn't tell. The voice was muffled, and the number was blocked."

"How much did they want for it?" I said.

"One-point-two mil."

When asked what her superiors said to that, she told me they just laughed and shook their heads. I thanked her for the heads-up and, before hanging up, told her I loved her.

"Be careful," was all she said.

After we disconnected, I thought about what I had just been told. The asking price was approximately half of what Professor Pendry had quoted, but still too rich for most people's blood, even a huge retailer like the Wine Emporium. *The thief must be getting awfully desperate,* I thought.

Back home in my office, I looked up the phone number to the Northern California Power Agency and got connected to the branch handling the Napa region. When I got through, I asked to speak with technical support.

"Can you tell me if there was a power outage in the Napa area around late May?" I said. "In the evening?"

I was informed that they were not allowed to give out that information to just anyone. When asked why, they said it was corporate policy.

That's rubbish, I thought. *People know when the power goes out.* I asked to speak to a supervisor, then explained that I was writing a story for *The St. Helena Star* about how reliable and responsible our state hydro system is. I wanted to explore how, in peak months like May, there are very few, if any, outages. When he got on the line, the supervisor bought it.

"Can you tell me if there was a power outage of any sort in the Napa region from, say, the Vallejo to the Calistoga area, at the end of May?" I said.

There was silence as he checked. He came back to say there were none at the end of May, but several earlier in the month—one on the sixteenth, around six in the evening, and another on the night of the twentieth, around nine.

"You're sure?" I said, jotting it down.

"Absolutely. We keep immaculate records."

I asked him one more thing—how most power transformers were controlled. He told me it was done by computer. I thanked him for his time, got his name for the supposed article, and hung up.

After disconnecting, I sat back, nodding. The light dimly shining in my brain was starting to glow brighter.

There was one hitch, though: Neither blackout took place during the dinner party when the wine went missing. Besides, wouldn't a complex security system like McCall's have a backup generator that would kick in if a power failure were detected?

I dialed McCall to ask. He wasn't happy to hear from me, but as it turns out, I was right. There was indeed a backup generator.

And what of the image of the wine still showing when the wine wasn't there? Even if the wine was lifted before the dinner party, the system was not set up for veiling to cover it up, unless a computer whiz kid like Johnny Spezzo could change that. After all, I *had* seen him solve in two minutes what I thought was an impossible problem on McCall's computer the night I first met him at the estate.

I searched the internet and called another security company, Williams & James Security Inc.

"Something like that has to be built into the system when created," I was told by Mr. Williams, one of the partners. "It simply cannot be done after the fact."

So much for that theory, I thought.

The next day, after spending some time working on that appraisal I had signed on to do, I called Ralph Wader and made an appointment to pop by his office and take a look at the blueprints for the house. He had them in a huge file marked "McCall." I pulled them out and spread them over his desk.

"Can I ask exactly what you're looking for?" he said, peering over my shoulder.

"Unless there was some other entrance into the house, the wine would have to have been removed through either the front or back door—pretty hard to do without being seen or recorded. Was this house built from the ground up?" I said, examining the blueprints.

"I don't really know. The person to ask is Sam Spezzo. He was the real estate developer who found the house for McCall."

"Then I guess you wouldn't know what, if anything, was on this site before the present dwelling was constructed," I said.

"Sorry, can't help you there, either."

I was hesitant to bother the Spezzos so soon after their son's death, but I needed this info to move along in my investigation. I dialed his number, and Sam picked up.

"How are you and the family holding up?" I said.

"It's slow going."

"I can only imagine," I said. "Listen, Mr. Spezzo, are you up to answering a few questions about Mr. McCall's missing wine? I'd completely understand if you said no."

He thought about it for a moment.

"Sure, why not?" he said. "It'll help take my mind off Johnny."

I asked him about McCall's property—specifically, if there was a pre-existing structure on the site.

"Yes—if I recall correctly, there was a structure of some sort there before McCall purchased it. I believe it was a winery that produced sparkling wine, but it was in such disrepair that it was basically gutted. McCall's house was designed and built by a Canadian firm."

"When you say 'gutted,' do you mean totally demolished, including the basement?" I said.

"I wouldn't swear my life on it," said Sam, "but if my memory serves me correctly, I don't recall any part of the previous substructure remaining."

I thanked Sam for his time, once again expressing my deepest sorrow for his loss.

Before leaving Wader's office, I had him make a photocopy of the basement blueprints. "I really don't know why you had to come here for blueprints," he said. "There's a set at the estate."

"Mr. McCall said there wasn't," I said.

"There is somewhere. I'm sure of it. You should ask Ms. Svenson. She was around when the house was being built and oversaw much of the work," Wader said, handing the blueprints to his secretary to copy.

The blueprint was so large, it had to be reproduced in four pieces and taped together. Once I had my copy, I called the Napa City-County Library to see if they had an archive there of historical Napa buildings, but was told they didn't. But they said that the San Francisco Public Library's main branch on Larkin Street had such an archive, so I headed over. The drive took about twenty minutes.

I found my way to the archives of historical buildings in Napa. I wasn't quite sure what I was looking for, but I had a hunch. As I went through aerial photos of historically significant homesteads in the area from the last hundred years, I came across one at the same address as McCall's home. It was very different than the structure today. There was a cross-reference to the Napa Valley Winery Association archives, so I followed the lead and found the reference. What I read was astonishing.

The previous structure was indeed a winery, with the house attached. It was called "Maison Raleigh" after the owner, a French immigrant, and was indeed a producer of bubbly in the Champagne tradition.

Now, here's the real interesting part: Just as in Champagne, France, where tunnels were carved into the chalk hills surrounding the wineries to cellar the aging bubbly, there were underground tunnels around the winery on this property in Napa.

I sat back in the chair I was occupying and rubbed my head. I'd bet my brown shoelaces that McCall's house still contained some of those tunnels or passages underneath, and that's how the wine exited.

In the same historical file was a rough schematic of the original dwelling, showing its tunnels and passageways. It wasn't very clear, but it would certainly be interesting to compare them to the blueprints of the existing house. I pulled out my copy of the present structure and sat it next to the rough schematic. They were very different, but you could see the logic behind the new design. From what I could make out, there were two possible passageways or tunnels that might still exist. One was off what was now the game room, and the other was off the laundry room.

I had thoroughly inspected the game room, because that's where the wine cellar and secret vault were. There was nothing there. However, I had never checked out the laundry room. I remembered passing it initially when I went down to the basement with McCall to examine the crime scene. It was huge, as I recalled.

I asked the librarian if he could make a copy of the historical schematics, but he said no. All historical documents of this nature were state-owned, and no copies or prints could be made without government approval. Since I wasn't about to contact the government, I would have to do without.

I drove back out to the estate to check out this discovery. Ms. Svenson was back on duty, but she looked like crap. When I asked how she was, she said she was fine, but she sure didn't look it. I asked how Emily was doing. She told me Emily had been in her room since the accident, barely eating and crying constantly. Not good!

As I was about to go down to the basement, I passed the living room and overheard Lambeck telling his boss he'd be back at about 7 p.m. Neither of them knew I was there. When Lambeck went up to his room, I followed, pretending to go to the washroom. Instead, I lurked outside his door. I heard him speaking with someone in his normal voice about meeting in about twenty-five minutes. I had no idea what it was about, but it seemed a good opportunity to tail him and see.

I decided to put my examination of the laundry room on hold. Going back downstairs and out to my car, I drove off the estate and parked in the same place I had when tailing Amos.

CHAPTER 22

Ten minutes passed, and then out drove Lambeck in a green Lincoln Continental. I followed at a good distance, changing lanes often so he wouldn't catch on. He headed south into Vallejo, then to the west side of town, to a little Italian restaurant called Vini's on Tennessee Street, near the waterfront, in the historic part of town. Although the area had undergone many changes, there were still historic buildings, lovely Victorian homes, and thriving businesses.

The restaurant itself was nothing to look at from the outside. It had a big glass window with the name "Vini's" painted in white in an arch, advertising "The Best Pizza in Town." A large green and red retractable awning was perched above it. It was a warm afternoon, and the front door was open.

Parking and exiting his car, Lambeck went inside. I parked up the street a bit, then walked to the restaurant and carefully peered in through the window. The inside held about eight small, round tables, covered in checkered tablecloths, and a small bar. Empty Italian wine bottles were lined up on the wainscoting around the perimeter. Photos of what I assumed were relatives of the owners back in Italy adorned the walls. The place looked like a typical family-run establishment. I could hear Italian being spoken through the open door. There was no sign of Lambeck.

All of a sudden, a door in the back of the place opened, and a heavy right out of *The Sopranos* came out, grabbed a bottle of wine from the bar, and went back in, closing the door behind him. *Lambeck must have gone in there, too*, I thought. I had to see what was going on.

I checked both sides of the establishment and found a skinny alleyway that led around back to a narrow laneway. I must have passed the kitchen, because the smells of garlic and tomato sauce were intoxicating.

I came around to the back of the building, where I found a small window and numerous trash cans lined up next to an open door. I could hear Lambeck's voice, and that of several others. They were speaking English. Very carefully and quietly, up between several cans, I shimmied up the wall to peer in. The scene I viewed was right out of a gangster flick.

There was a round, wooden table with wooden chairs. Four men, a few smoking cigars, sat playing cards. One of them was Lambeck. On the table were several bottles of wine, a quart of some clear spirit, half-filled glasses, piles of cash, and ashtrays. Sitting off to the side, talking on a cellphone, was the guy who had come out to retrieve the wine. He looked to be in his forties, tall, well-built, and clean-shaven. There was another guy, equally menacing, similar build and age—perhaps a little older—with a mustache, reading a newspaper as he leaned against a bureau of some sort. The air was thick with cigar smoke.

The three chaps playing cards with Lambeck didn't look too kosher either. One was about sixty, with graying hair and glasses, dressed in a white shirt and dark slacks. The second appeared to be older, maybe in his mid to late seventies, with greased-back, receding, brownish-gray hair. He was garbed in gray suit pants, a white short-sleeved shirt, and a gray hat. He looked like an older version of George Raft, the actor who played a gangster in all those movies in the thirties and forties. The final dude, around the same age, with curly, gray, thinning hair, sported a beige polo shirt and brown pants. None of them looked like a choirboy.

As they played cards, they chatted about what I can only assume was business. They asked Lambeck numerous questions about money issues, none of which seemed relevant to my case. At one point, though, one of the older fellows, named Larry, talked about getting money owed them from a gambling debt. I heard the other older chap, called Dom, say they had the guy worked over pretty good as a warning. If he didn't pay up, he'd be "worm chowder."

Hearing that scared the crap out of me, and I staggered back, knocking over a garbage can. The voices within stopped. I heard one of the older guys say—I'm guessing to the younger guys not playing cards—to go check it out. I turned and ran like the wind, getting out of there before the hoods could make it outside and catch me. I raced back to my car, got in, and sat there, petrified. My pulse was racing so fast I could hardly catch my breath, and I was sweating fear. *Holy mother of God! They're bad news for sure*, I thought. Wouldn't want to owe those guys any money!

Then—a lightning bolt! I finally remembered that bit of info I had recorded but couldn't recall. When I was over at her place, Patricia had mentioned that Horace was playing poker with money he didn't have with Lambeck and some of his buddies. *Geez, could these guys have been them? Is it Horace who they worked over? Is it Horace who might become worm chowder?*

I immediately called Georgey, told him what Patricia had said (but not what I had just seen), and suggested they put a police officer outside Horace's room at the hospital, just in case. It then occurred to me again that, if Johnny Spezzo was indeed involved with the mob in the theft, and these were the guys, maybe he somehow pissed them off, and his death, then, was no accident.

When I calmed down enough to drive, I headed north, back up to the estate.

CHAPTER 23

After being let in by Ms. Svenson, I made my way down to the basement in search of the laundry room. It was as huge as I remembered. There were numerous industrial frontloading washing machines and five heavy duty industrial dryers. In the middle of the room was a long table, used, I supposed, for folding laundry. On one wall was a steaming machine, the kind professional cleaners use. On another was a big pressing machine. Next to the table was an ironing board with an iron and, off to one side, a shelf holding all kinds of cleaning paraphernalia. The walls were paneled, not unlike in the game room. I started looking about on the paneling, and then behind the steamer, pressing machine, and shelf, for some indication of a doorway or opening.

All of a sudden, I heard something behind me. Turning around, there stood Ms. Svenson.

"What are you doing?" she said, arms folded across her chest. "Perhaps I can be of assistance?" She must have thought I'd gone to the basement to examine the vault area. She was clearly surprised to find me in the laundry room.

I thought fast. "Mr. McCall said there was some wiring to the security system through here," I said.

Ms. Svenson looked at me strangely, and I wasn't sure she bought it.

"The main power source and electrical box are in the security control center," she said. "Come with me."

I had no alternative but to follow her into the control center down the hall. I pretended to examine the wiring and connections. She stood over me the whole time.

"I can't see anything unusual," I said, rubbing my hands together to wipe off any excess dust.

I didn't know if Svenson was trying to deter me deliberately or just to help. Either way, I would have to sneak down here another time alone and check more thoroughly.

From there, we headed back upstairs, where I ran into McCall.

"Sir, are you aware that Emily hasn't come out of her room since Johnny's funeral?" I said.

"I'm well aware of that, Robins, and I'm quite worried about her."

"Can I ask when the last time was you actually saw or spoke to her?"

He thought about it for a moment and looked as if he was counting days.

"I'm not exactly sure," he said, sounding worried. "I'd better check on her."

Both Ms. Svenson and I followed him up to her room, and he knocked on the door. There was no answer.

"Emily, are you okay?" he called through the door. No answer.

McCall knocked louder.

"Emily, please, are you okay?" he said. Nothing!

Trying the door, he found it locked. He turned to Ms. Svenson.

"Ursula, use your master key and open this door immediately," he said, starting to get frantic.

Ms. Svenson fumbled in her apron for keys.

"Hurry, Ursula!" McCall said, growing more frantic.

"I don't have them."

McCall started rattling the door in an attempt to open it. He even threw his body against it in desperation. The door wouldn't budge.

"Stand back, sir," I said, backing up and charging the door to break it down.

I bounced off the door like a sponge ball off a brick wall, hurting my shoulder.

"For God's sakes, try again!" McCall said, almost beside himself. "Hurry!"

Again, I backed up and charged the door. This time it gave way, the lock snapping and the door swinging open. We ran into the room.

Emily was lying in bed, unconscious. In one hand was an empty bottle of sleeping pills; in the other, a note that simply read, "I can't live without Johnny."

"Oh no!" McCall screamed.

I gave her a couple of light smacks on the face to see if she could be revived, but had no luck.

"Call 9-1-1 immediately," I said.

Ms. Svenson dialed the number. Within ten minutes, an ambulance arrived.

McCall insisted on riding along in the ambulance to Queen of the Valley Medical Center. Ms. Svenson stayed behind while I followed in my own car.

In the emergency waiting room, McCall paced up and down like a wild cat caught in a cage. He checked his watch every two minutes, looking completely distraught. Every time someone in a white lab coat came out of the emergency room, he lunged forward at them, expecting news about Emily.

"Would you like a coffee or something, sir?" I said, trying to calm him down.

"No. Nothing."

He tried sitting down, but that didn't last long. Soon, he was up pacing again. This went on for about fifty-five minutes until, finally, the attending doctor stepped out.

"Who's family here?" he said, looking at the two of us.

McCall stepped forward, bracing himself for the worst.

The doctor took him about twenty feet down the corridor, out of my earshot. I prepared myself for bad news. But when McCall shook the doctor's hand, the jubilation on his face told me Emily would be okay.

McCall returned to me.

"It was a little touch and go there for a while," said McCall, "but they saved her. She's going to be fine."

"Thank God," I said with a sigh.

"They're going to keep her in the hospital a few days for observation. She'll be moved to a private room."

"Do you want a lift back to the estate?" I said.

"No, I'm going to stay."

As I left, I heard him call Ms. Svenson to tell her.

As serious and sad as the situation was, I couldn't help but think that this was the first time I'd ever felt sympathy for McCall. Even when he originally had told me that his wife was dead, he had showed no emotion. I had started to think he was a robot, or an alien. *So he's human after all,* I thought.

CHAPTER 24

I t was early evening when I made it back to San Francisco. It had been quite a day so far, and I needed a drink. I stopped by the Gull en route for a quick one. Then I popped in on Sadie to see how she was holding up. She was surprised to see me, but I was surprised, too.

"My God, you need a cane?" I said. She was now using a cane to get around.

"Quite the fashion statement, don't you think, Woody?" Sadie said, awkwardly attempting to pose with it. "Should come in designer colors and patterns!"

She was making light of it, I know, but I could tell by her face that she was experiencing a heck of a lot of pain. I was very concerned about her.

"We'll figure this out. I guarantee it," I said, putting my arms around her.

Deep down, I was praying that I would. It was all the more reason to stick with this case despite the danger. The fee would solve Sadie's problems.

"How's the case coming along?" Sadie said. "Is it almost wrapped up?"

"Almost," was all I said.

I sure as hell didn't tell her about spying on the "Sopranos." Nor did I mention Emily's attempt at suicide. I had learned my lesson the other day.

"Please be careful, Woody," she said as I left.

Finally, at home, I sat down in my office before retiring. I tried desperately to remember all the facts and notations I had earlier made on my tape recorder. My memory was simply not built for long-term storage.

Cleaning out my briefcase, I came across my scribbled notes containing the names I'd found on the gambling receipts in Lambeck's drawer. "Oh crap!" I exclaimed. "Little Larry" Dentico and Dominick "Quiet Dom"

Cirillo. I remembered the other men calling the two older mugs at the Italian restaurant Larry and Dom.

Googling their names again, I found one sentence that jumped out at me: "Little Larry and Quiet Dom are trustworthy old-timers known to do their bosses' bidding with little fear of opposition from within or outside the family."

Now I was really scared.

Once again, I slept poorly, kept awake by visions of Little Larry and Quiet Dom catching me and fitting me for cement overshoes. I pondered whether I should tell Georgey that these were the guys who possibly beat up Horace Botner, but I really had no proof as of yet. I also had no proof that they were involved with the theft of the wine. But there was no doubt they were into other bad stuff. I mean, they were the mob! Racketeering, gambling, theft, and even murder were, I'm sure, everyday pastimes.

In the morning, I called Georgey to give him their names. The call went to his voice mail, so I left a message. If they were indeed involved, I hoped he wouldn't do anything immediately, like move in on them, because it might hinder my investigation. I asked that he call me back when he had a chance.

Whatever happened from now on, I'd have to step cautiously.

After that, I called the estate to see how Emily was doing. Ms. Svenson told me that she was still in the hospital, but coming along. The doctors said she would come home the next day.

I was still feeling particularly stupid, unhappy, and ashamed about my behavior the other night with Julia. I had really hurt her feelings. I missed her, so I called to see if she wanted to meet for a coffee. I didn't know what kind of reception to expect. Fortunately, she agreed. I met her at noon just outside her office, and we headed to the Bean Hut, a nearby café.

As we sipped a couple of cappuccinos outside, Julia was sweet as usual, but there was definitely an unspoken tension between us. I asked if there were any more calls about the missing wine, and she said no.

We were sipping our coffees when I heard, "Hey, Julia, how are you?"

It was a tall, good-looking guy, with blond, curly hair, who Julia obviously knew.

"Fancy running into you here! You look lovely today," he said.

"Thanks," she said, looking over at me and acting a little uncomfortable. "Roger, this is Woody. Woody, Roger. Roger works in the legal department of our Oakland office."

We silently acknowledged each other.

"Tell me, Julia, did I happen to leave my sweater at your place the other day?" Roger said.

My ears perked up.

"No," she said, looking more uncomfortable.

Seeing the questioning look on my face, she immediately added, "Roger dropped some work off at my office the other day."

I wasn't sure if she was telling the truth or not, and I started to feel bad, as a wave of jealousy enveloped me. They chatted for a few more minutes before Roger excused himself.

"Take care, Julia. Nice meeting you, Woody," he said, walking away.

We sat there in an uncomfortable silence for a few minutes, both staring down into our coffees. I thought about questioning her about it further, but decided not to. It would probably only make a scene.

While sitting there, I noticed a folded-up Oakland-specific newspaper in her open purse, turned to the classifieds. From what I could see, it was the part with apartments for rent, and several were circled in ink.

"Looking for a new place to live?" I said, reaching out and touching her hand.

"You know my lease is up shortly," said Julia.

Not knowing what to say at this point, I asked what was wrong with the old place.

"Just too many memories there," she said.

"But in Oakland?" I said, very surprised, wondering if it had anything at all to do with this Roger guy.

"I need a change."

What she really needs is to get away from me, I thought.

After we finished, I walked Julia back to the office in silence. Just as we were about to part, she turned to me.

"Look, Woody—this doesn't seem to be working out. I don't think we should see each other anymore," she said.

My heart sank.

"Don't you love me?" I said, taking her hands in mine.

"I do. I really do, but it's simply not enough," said Julia with tears in her eyes. "You don't trust me. The expression on your face when I was talking to Roger said it all over again. I can't go on like this."

A little voice inside of me kept saying, *Ask her to move in. Ask her to move in.* But I couldn't bring myself to say it.

"But I love you," I said, fighting to hold back tears.

"Do you, Woody?" she said, staring at me with those big, beautiful, tearful eyes.

With that, she told me to take care of myself and gave me a farewell peck on the cheek, then turned and walked away.

I stood there, stunned, feeling as if she had reached into my chest and ripped out my heart. Tears trickled down my cheeks. *Why couldn't you ask her to move in?* The question kept replaying in my brain. *You love her. What's your problem?*

The truth of the matter was I didn't know why.

I drove home, crying all the way. Once inside, I called Sadie for some comfort.

"You poor baby. I'm so sorry," she said. "I'll be right over."

But I immediately talked her out of the idea. She was in no shape to go gallivanting around, even to console a lovesick puppy like me. We just chatted for a while on the phone.

"So what are you going to do now?" she said.

"I don't know."

"You could come and stay with me for a couple days."

The idea was tempting, but I really wasn't up to it.

"Thanks for the offer, Sadie, but I'll take a pass. I have lots of work to do. I'll just throw myself into that," I said.

I *did* have lots of work to do, but whether I could concentrate on it was another story. If the truth be known, I didn't feel like doing anything. I just wanted to be alone.

"Well, if you need me, I'm right here. I love you," she said before hanging up.

What to do now that my love was gone? I holed up in the house the rest of the day, licking my wounds. Almost everything I looked at reminded me of Julia: my selection of hats on the rack that she always kidded me about, the CD of Sinatra that we danced slow to so many times, and the photo of me last Halloween, where she convinced me to dress like a girl, complete with wig, stockings, and makeup. What really hurt was the bed where we spent so many endless hours cuddling.

Just before turning in (not that I would be able to sleep), I received a call from Georgey.

"You know, the guys whose names you left me are real heavy players," he said. "You think they had something to do with Botner's beating?"

I told him I wasn't sure, but it couldn't hurt to take precautions.

"You want to stay as far away from guys like this as possible."

"No shit, Sherlock," I said, quite straightforwardly.

"You sound funny. Are you okay?"

"I'm fine, just tired," I said.

"Hey, how'd you come up with those guys' names anyway?"

I lied and said Horace Botner had mentioned them before his beating. Besides, Horace was comatose now and couldn't verify it. I didn't want to tell Georgey just yet that they might be involved with the wine theft, too. After all, I still had no proof.

Georgey had checked out Joe Philips's wife, as well as pulled all the employee and customer records. He'd narrowed the suspects list to three people who were both brunette and left-handed. Two had alibis that were corroborated. The other, Jeremy Cross, who worked for the auction house, had gone away on vacation after the murder and would be back in few days. The timing of his vacation seemed suspicious. Perhaps he was avoiding the police. "He could be our guy," Georgey said.

He also said he had starting looking into McCall's staff and family, but had yet to question them.

"See if you can find out if Ursula Svenson, McCall's housekeeper, is a legal immigrant," I said. "And see if Johnny Spezzo's death really was an accident."

"Do you think there's some connection between Spezzo and these mob guys?" Georgey said.

I told him I didn't know, but it couldn't hurt to check it out. I knew that whatever I was looking into would be uncovered by Georgey, too. This investigation of mine needed to pick up steam, because once any of that stuff was out in the open, it would definitely hinder my efforts to keep things secret. That the suspects didn't know what I knew certainly worked in my favor. Besides, if Georgey, in his investigation, actually recovered the wine, McCall might not pay me. I needed that money for Sadie.

I tried to sleep, but it eluded me. I was heartbroken.

CHAPTER 25

The next day, I decided that the only way I could manage losing Julia was, as I had said to Sadie, to throw myself into work big-time. Donning a pair of baggy, dark, pleated pants, a collarless, navy blue shirt, a pair of brogues, and a black fedora, I set out for the estate. I still needed to search that laundry room. I hoped Ms. Svenson was otherwise occupied. Sure enough, when I arrived, Lambeck let me in. Svenson was nowhere about, and when Lambeck went to do something elsewhere in the house, I made my way down to the laundry room. I started to search, but suddenly there was a voice from behind me.

"Can I be of some service, sir?"

Turning around, I stared at Lambeck, raising his left eyebrow.

I felt like saying, "Yeah, get lost," but didn't. Once again, I had to fabricate a story as to why I was down there. I used the same line on him as I had used on Svenson: something about checking out wiring to the security system that ran through the laundry room. Lambeck led me to the security control center, and like Svenson, he wouldn't let me be.

Geez, I just can't catch a break. For folks who only go down in the basement either to retrieve wine or clean, both Lambeck and Svenson seemed to be there a lot. *Maybe they're both aware of what I'm looking for,* I thought.

"You don't need to stand over me, Mr. Lambeck. I can check this out on my own," I said.

"Mr. McCall told me to stay close to you in case you need any help."

I didn't believe him for a minute, but seeing as I had no choice, I returned to the main floor, finding McCall in the kitchen nursing a cappuccino and talking to Ms. Svenson. I was tempted to ask him if he did indeed tell Lambeck to shadow me, but I knew what the answer would be.

Instead, I inquired as to Emily's condition. Emily, I learned, had arrived home earlier in the morning and was resting in her room.

"She's not alone, is she?" I said.

"Until she's better, I have a private nurse staying with her around the clock," said McCall.

I asked about her headspace. McCall said it was no better, and he was considering having her see a psychiatrist to help her deal with her grief.

Then, I took him aside and asked him for a favor—to send both Svenson and Lambeck away on a job together, shopping or something like that, so they couldn't bother me while I searched the laundry room.

"The laundry room? That's plain stupid."

When I explained to him why, he was still uncooperative.

"That's ridiculous. I'll just tell them not to bother you," McCall said, putting his hands on his hips.

I asked him not to, as I didn't want them to know I was down there. After some persuading, he finally agreed and sent them off to pick out new tiles for the front hallway he was contemplating redoing. He said that, since both of them would be involved in cleaning them, it would be best if they went together to choose. He even got Amos to drive them. Once they left, I started for the basement stairs, only to be interrupted by McCall.

"Look, Robins, this investigation of yours seems to be going absolutely nowhere quickly," he said. "You have exactly five days to solve it, and then I'm calling in someone else." He stared coldly into my eyes.

I didn't know what to say. As much as I wanted things to progress faster, putting the screws to me this way wasn't going to help.

"But, sir—"

He stopped me by putting up his hand and shaking his head. He then turned and walked away.

I stood there dazed for a moment. The attitude, the stare, the insistence on not discussing it, the abrupt dismissal—it was uncanny. It really was like being with my father.

But my thoughts turned to Sadie. If I couldn't solve this case and get the substantial finder's fee, she would not be able to have the operation she so desperately needed. Panic started to rear its ugly head. I was getting it from all sides. First Julia, now McCall!

After calming down, I convinced myself that I could solve this case in the allotted timeframe. I just needed to focus—and if the second threatening letter and slashing of my tire was any indication, I *was* getting close. Back down to the laundry room I scurried. But searching every possible wall behind all the equipment revealed no evidence of a passageway.

"Damn!" I screamed in frustration, banging my hand down on the table in the middle of the room. *There's got to be something down here*, I kept thinking. *I'd swear it.*

I went upstairs and out to my car, then headed back to San Francisco. Stopping quickly at home to pick up the blueprints of the house, I returned to the Napa history section of the library. Examining the schematic of the original house, I looked to see if I had indeed miscalculated somehow. If I had, I couldn't see it. I kept going over both plans, but saw nothing. It was frustrating.

Leaving the library, I headed home. I checked my answering machine in the office, hoping—praying, I guess—that Julia might have changed her mind about us and left a message. Sadly, nothing from her.

Suddenly, my office phone rang. It was Georgey. He told me that he had looked into Johnny Spezzo's death and found that it was indeed an accident. No evidence of foul play. I asked if the police had found anything unusual in his car that might lead to the wine.

"All that was found were some maps, a first-aid kit, and some brochures on adoption agencies."

"Adoption agencies?" I said, surprised.

"What's so strange about that? Lots of people adopt kids."

Were Johnny and Emily planning on adopting a child once married? If so, that could mean that either he or she was infertile.

"One more thing," Georgey said. "I couldn't find any evidence whatsoever of Ursula Svenson legally immigrating to the United States, so more than likely she's an undocumented alien. Just before Georgey hung up, he said, "Watch your butt!" Believe me, I had every intention of doing so.

I again pulled out the blueprints of McCall's basement and kept going over them. I knew there was something I was missing, but I just couldn't see it. They were typical architect's prints, showing rooms, corridors, measurements, etc.

"Wait a minute!" I said, jumping up from my seat. Looking a little closer at the measurements, I realized my mistake. *Of course! How could I have been so stupid?*

The measurements of the present structure were in meters. Sam Spezzo had said the McCall house was designed and built by a Canadian company. They used the metric system. The original schematic was obviously done by Americans way back when, and most likely in feet and yards. That could be it. *That* must *be it!* I thought. If so, that would put all my calculations off by some thirty or so feet—probably to the left.

Looking again at the present structure's blueprints of the basement put a possible passageway in the home gym.

Just to be sure, I went back to the library and checked. Sure enough, I was right. The original schematic was in feet. Now to check it out!

I drove back up to the estate excited by this newfound info. Both Svenson and Lambeck were there, talking to the boss. How I was going to go back into the basement without either Svenson or Lambeck coming down was another story. When McCall was alone, I asked him if he ever used the gym downstairs.

"Again with the stupid questions, Robins?" he said, shaking his head.

From his response, I guessed not. Both Svenson and Lambeck were hanging around like vultures. I needed them out of the way, but how? I couldn't ask McCall to keep them busy again. He was already disenchanted with me.

Suddenly, Denise came downstairs. I hadn't seen her since Johnny's funeral.

"Denise, a minute, please!" I said.

"What do you want?" she said. "I'm busy."

Thinking quickly, I came up with a story: "As I was just driving in, I noticed the stable door open down at the barn, and there seemed to be some smoke billowing out. Maybe you should check it out—with Ms. Svenson and Mr. Lambeck."

At first, she looked at me weirdly, almost as if to say I was full of it. However, I knew that, with her love of horses, she couldn't afford to take that chance.

"Ursula, Michael," she said, "come with me."

The three of them scurried off.

I whipped downstairs to the gym, full of Nautilus equipment and wet and dry saunas. First, I looked at the bare walls, finding nothing. Then I checked behind all the Nautilus equipment. Nothing there, either. Then, I tried to calculate the distance based on where I thought the laundry room entrance would be, and that brought me right in front of the dry sauna. It was built right up to the wall, so I couldn't look behind. When I went inside the paneled unit, I checked the back. Because of the paneled lines, I couldn't see any visible break in the wall, but as I tried, I tripped over a step up and bounced off the wall.

All of a sudden, a seam about five feet high by four feet wide appeared. It looked like a small doorway. I tried moving it with my hands, but it wouldn't budge. Taking out my car keys, I jimmied it open enough to peer inside. It was dark, but the little bit of light from the sauna told me it went on for quite a distance.

Eureka! I've found it!

I knew I didn't have enough time to explore it properly. Once Denise et al discovered there was nothing going on at the stable, they'd be back. I quickly closed the door, stepping outside the sauna. As I looked back at where the doorway was and which wall it was on, I tried to get my bearings as to which side of the house it faced. It appeared to be off the back somewhere. But more important now was, where exactly did it come out? In my research on the schematic of the previous dwelling, I had noticed that some of the tunnels went for great distances, as they often did in Champagne, France.

I made it back upstairs just in time. Denise, Svenson, and Lambeck came storming into the house, cursing.

"There was nothing of the sort going on at the stable. You're seeing things," Denise said curtly, looking at me as if I was nuts.

"I'm sorry. I must have been mistaken," I said.

Both Svenson and Lambeck glared at me.

What I really needed was to have a walk around the house to try to calculate where that passageway came out, but I had too many folks suspicious of me at the moment and I knew my searching would not go unnoticed. It would have to wait for another time—but then I thought about McCall's ultimatum. I didn't have time. I needed answers now.

I walked around to the back of the house. Standing by the pool, I tried to visualize where the sauna was. If my calculations were correct, it would come off the house somewhere under the patio. Where it went from there was anybody's guess.

As I stood there, looking at the back of the house, my eye caught Lambeck, standing on the small balcony off his room on the second floor. He just stared at me. I don't know if he wondered what I was doing or if he knew. I tried to ignore him as I looked around, but I could feel his eyes on me. *Don't you have anything else to do?* I thought. It gave me the willies.

Continuing on regardless, I carefully walked the area of the property that ran off behind the pool, looking for anything that might show evidence of a passageway. I really didn't know what I was looking for. Was it a cave, a hole in the ground, a doorway? It could be anything, and anywhere.

After about an hour of unsuccessful hunting, I came back out by the pool area. I looked up to Lambeck's balcony. Gone. At that point, I gave up in frustration and headed back to San Fran.

I had figured out that there *was* a secret passageway or tunnel from the house, which was most probably the route the wine took to get out. Where it actually came out was still a mystery, as was, of course, who executed the theft—and, perhaps more importantly, why. I kept trying to recall bits of info I had noted on my tape recorder. Something was probably there that would point me in the right direction.

I thought about the possibility of Amos stealing the wine, with Denise's help. If it was for the money, why was there no ransom demanded? And why would Denise help someone steal from her own father? Although her relationship with McCall wasn't what I would call stellar, it was still a far cry better than Emily's. Still, judging from what I had heard in the bar when I tailed Amos, her guilt was a good possibility, but I had no actual way of proving it at this point.

Then there was the theory of Emily helping Johnny Spezzo lift the wine. Johnny and Touchstone could have been in cahoots—but to what end? There was no ransom note, and neither Touchstone nor Johnny seemed to lack funds. Touchstone appeared to have a very lucrative business, and Johnny was from a well-to-do family. And what of Emily's involvement? Maybe to get back at her father for, in her mind, allowing her mother to die? Revenge *can* drive a person to extremes.

What about Horace Botner, an addicted gambler, drunk, and overall boob? He could have stolen the wine to repay a gambling debt, especially if it was to the mob.

Then enter Michael Lambeck, a two-bit actor, crook, and Mafia associate. Was he a plant to steal the wine for them?

Finally, there was Ms. Svenson, a strange lady who appeared to be in this country illegally, and for all intents and purposes knew the McCall house better than anyone. But as for motivation, I couldn't think of anything.

An outsider couldn't possibly have orchestrated this theft without someone on the inside.

And what of the murder of poor Mr. Philips? How did that play into the scenario?

The clock was ticking for me on this case, and my head was dizzy with info. I needed a rest. Looking at myself in my bathroom mirror, I realized I looked like crap. I hadn't slept properly in days, and my heart ached. Deciding to take a light sedative, I got into bed and tried to sleep.

I must have dozed off, and I don't know what I was dreaming about, but I suddenly bolted upright in bed.

"Holy moly!" I cried. "The stone bridge!" It hit me like a bus.

I remembered noting it on my recorder. When Emily and I had gone for that stroll after dinner the first night and stopped on the stone bridge to watch the bullfrog, I had noticed footprints in the mud along the bank. I had completely forgotten about them.

I needed to check under that bridge.

CHAPTER 26

The next morning, I went back out to McCall's, but didn't go up to the house. Instead, I drove around to the cottage and parked my wheels there. I then ventured on foot along the path to the stone bridge. Climbing down onto the bank and stooping under the bridge, I looked for some sort of entrance on the side closest to the house. The wall was covered with overgrown moss, but there *was* something—a small, old wooden door with bars on it. I pushed it open, and it led into a long tunnel heading back in the direction of the house.

"This is it!" I said. It was extremely dark, and I didn't have a flashlight, or I would have ventured down to see where it led. (I made a mental note, not that I would remember, to stash a flashlight in my car's glove compartment for future situations like this.)

So whoever stole the wine could have removed it through the sauna in the basement, along the passageway, and out here to a waiting car by the cottage, and nobody would have been the wiser.

But how the wine got out of the vault to the sauna was still a mystery.

Returning to my car, I wiped the mud off my shoes as best I could and drove around to the main house. Going inside, I ran directly into Ms. Svenson. She stared down at my muddy shoes.

"Been doing some puddle-jumping?" she said with an angry look on her face.

"Yeah," was all I said.

"Well, take those damn things off. I just washed the floors."

I know she wondered why my feet were all muddy. It hadn't rained in almost a week. I felt like a little kid being scolded for getting dirty, but I obliged.

Just then, my cell phone rang. It was Georgey. He told me he had uncovered some interesting stuff about Michael Lambeck and his link to the mob.

"It isn't even his real name," Georgey said.

"I know that."

"You knew that and you didn't say? That's called withholding evidence, my boy," he said, sounding really ticked off. "Does McCall know who this guy really is?"

"I highly doubt it, and I would really appreciate you not bringing it up and making it public knowledge just yet." I didn't want Georgey blowing any chance of my solving the case.

"This is a murder investigation, you understand," he said. "It takes precedence over a theft."

"I'm begging you, Georgey. Just hold off for a few more days, at least until my time on this case runs out."

"I don't know, Woody. Did you know there's a warrant out for his arrest in New York State?"

I didn't know that, but I wasn't surprised to hear it.

"Please. I'm on my knees here," I said.

"All right, all right, I can't stand to see a grown man beg. But just a couple days, and that's it! You got it?"

Changing the subject, I asked if he had managed to contact that Jeremy Cross fellow from Philips's office, but the guy still wasn't back from vacation.

Hanging up with Georgey, I pondered my next move. As I went by the kitchen, I heard a voice that seemed to be talking on the phone. It was vague, but as I moved into the kitchen, it got louder. It was coming from just outside the open patio doors, by the herb garden. Sneaking up closer, I could make out Denise's voice.

"So the guy is willing to meet our price?"

She listened for a moment.

"That's great. When is the deal going down?" she said.

More silence.

"This afternoon? What time? . . . Look, I'll meet up with you in about a half hour at the garage," she said, looking at her watch.

Geez, this could be it, I thought.

I hustled from the kitchen and out to my car, where I sat, waiting for Denise to emerge. In about five minutes, out she came. I pretended to be talking on my cell phone as she passed me by and headed for her silver Beamer. I waited until she was a good distance ahead before putting my car in gear and following.

I tailed her north into the town of Oakville, to a dingy little garage. Parking a good distance away, I removed the binoculars I'd put in my glove compartment so I could see.

Denise got out of her car and went into the garage. A minute or two later, she emerged with a small package or envelope in her hand and a guy beside her. Focusing my binocs, I recognized the guy as the same one playing pool with Amos at his bar.

Holy moly!

Denise then got back into her car and drove north, to Rutherford—to Amos's house. I followed at a safe distance and stopped a good distance away. Through my binocs, I saw her exit the car with the package and take it into the house. A few minutes later, she came out without the package and got into her car. I actually contemplated sticking around after Denise left and sneaking into Amos's house to check out its content, but breaking and entering was not a good idea. Denise started back to the estate in Napa, so I followed her there instead.

Parking a good distance up the driveway to the house, I saw her get out of her car, look around to see if anyone was watching, and head for the garage, probably to inform Amos that the deal had transpired. Within a few minutes, she emerged again and went into the house.

I tried to figure out what had gone down. Could she and Amos have managed to find a buyer for the wine? What was the small package she dropped off at his place—money? It was very suspicious.

I pulled up to the front of the house and parked my wheels. Just as I was getting out of the car, my cell phone rang.

CHAPTER 27

A screaming, irate woman was on the other end of the line. At first, I didn't even recognize the voice, but then I got it.

"Julia, is that you?" I said, immediately concerned.

"You bastard. It's all your fault!" she yelled.

"Whoa, what are you talking about?"

"You put my life in jeopardy!" she said.

"Get a hold of yourself and tell me what you're talking a—"

"These two big gorillas . . .!" Her voice trailed off into curses.

It took a few minutes for her to control herself long enough to spill what had happened. Apparently, she was leaving her apartment when these two big guys approached her in the hallway, roughed her up a little, and said that if I didn't lay off of this case, they would kill her.

"I told them we weren't together, but they didn't care," she said.

I asked where Julia was at that moment, and she said inside her apartment.

"Pack a bag, take a taxi over to Sadie's place, and stay there," I said.

She fought me at first, but her fear got the better of her and she agreed. Hanging up, I called Sadie and filled her in on the situation, telling her I was on my way. I then called Georgey and told him what had happened. I asked that a police officer be placed outside Sadie's place for protection.

Within an hour, I was at Sadie's apartment. A police officer was already on guard outside. Julia was furious. She couldn't stop ranting.

"I kept telling them we weren't together anymore, but they just wouldn't listen," she said.

"I'm so sorry, Julia," I kept saying over and over.

I tried to hug her, but she just pushed me away.

"It's a damn good thing I didn't have something to hit them with, 'cause I would have crowned them," she said, shaking her head.

After several more minutes of carrying on, she started to settle down somewhat. Sadie pulled a bottle of brandy out of the liquor cabinet and poured us three healthy shots. Within a half hour, Julia was calmer, but still extremely ticked off at me.

"Can you describe the two guys who threatened you?" I said, wondering if it was the same two who were at the poker game.

"They were big, mean . . ." Her voice trailed off. "It all happened so quickly."

She was still shaken up. Perhaps she would be better able to provide a proper description later.

Georgey called on my cell phone to make sure the cop was there and Julia was okay. He said he'd managed to reach that Jeremy Cross fellow from Philips's office and was going out to question him. He wanted to know if I wanted to tag along. I wasn't sure if I should leave the girls alone after what had happened, but Sadie took me aside and convinced me to go and not to worry. They would be fine. The cop was standing guard just outside the door, and besides, it would be a good idea to give Julia some space. Julia, of course, could stay as long as needed. Sadie said she would take care of her.

But who's going to take care of Sadie? I thought. Even with a cane, she could barely move. But Julia could help Sadie out as well.

Somewhat reluctantly, I agreed to meet Georgey. Cross lived near Sadie's—in the Inner Richmond part of town, an interesting ethnic community with many great and inexpensive restaurants. As I drove over to Inner Richmond, the intensity and danger of this case began to hit home.

Threatening me is one thing, but threatening the woman I love is going too far.

Arriving at the address Georgey had given me, I parked behind his car, where he was sitting, waiting for me. The neighborhood was quaint, with a combination of grand old homes, smaller stuccoed ones, and numerous Chinese eateries. Children played carelessly on the street. Georgey asked how Julia was doing, and I told him she was still extremely shaken up.

Knocking on the front door of one of the smaller houses, we were greeted by a dark-haired, middle-aged woman who I assumed was Cross's wife. She invited us in. The place was simply furnished, with a colonial-style couch and side chair, round wooden coffee table, and oak dining set with four captain's chairs. We were asked to sit down.

"Jeremy will be right with you," the woman said as she left.

A few minutes passed, and we could hear a man's voice in the kitchen talking with the woman. We then heard a strange, squeaky rolling noise, and we braced ourselves for the guy's appearance.

A nicely dressed man in his early fifties with brown hair appeared in the doorway. Georgey and I looked at each other with complete surprise, and then back at the man. The guy was in a wheelchair. He was a paraplegic.

"Are you Jeremy Cross?" Georgey said, a confused look on his face.

"Yes," said the man.

"And you work for Bonham & Butterfields?"

"Sure do," he said, cocking his head to one side. "I'm the bookkeeper," he said, "and I only work two days a week in the afternoon."

It almost seemed moot to proceed any further. The guy seemed frail. He could barely control his wheelchair. The concept of him somehow overpowering a man and killing him with a bung mallet seemed beyond plausibility. There had been no indication anywhere that this guy was a paraplegic—and with no criminal record or mug shot, why would there be? You would have thought that someone might have mentioned to Georgey that Cross was disabled.

Nonetheless, Georgey continued. I suppose weirder things have happened.

When asked where he was on the morning of Philips's death, Cross said he was at home, and his live-in caregiver, the woman with him, could testify to that. She did. Georgey also asked if he could think of anyone who might have disliked Philips enough to kill him. The guy said no.

"He was a quiet, well-respected man," said Cross. "He'll be sorely missed."

We thanked Cross for his time and left. Outside at our cars, I asked Georgey what his next move was, and he told me he was heading out to McCall's Napa estate to question his staff and family. *I should come along*, I thought. While Georgey occupied them with his interrogation, I could do some more snooping.

En route, I called Sadie to see how things were going. She said Julia was still shaken up, but was now taking a nap.

I wasn't entirely sure having Julia stay with my aunt was a good idea, seeing as she had broken up with me. I didn't want either Sadie or Julia feeling uncomfortable. But Sadie assured me that I had done the right thing. "It might even help mend your relationship," she said.

I really wasn't thinking in those terms. I was just concerned for her safety because I loved her. Okay, so I was feeling guilty as well, because she wouldn't be in this mess if it weren't for me. Either way, I felt better knowing that she was in good hands.

CHAPTER 28

We drove through a brief but heavy rain shower, and before I knew it, we were out at the estate.

"Geez, look at this spread," Georgey said as he got out of his car. "Worth a few bucks, eh?"

Inside the house, I introduced Georgey to McCall. The boss was expecting him. What he wasn't expecting was me coming along for the ride. Taking me aside, he said, with disdain in his eyes, "Why are you here . . . again?"

I told him I was still investigating the theft. According to his ultimatum, I still had another few days left.

Setting up in the library, Georgey had McCall send in each member of the staff individually. He started with Lambeck. Meanwhile, I went into the kitchen for a glass of water. While doing so, I heard something that sounded like mumbling from the adjoining pantry. Going up to the doorway and peering in, I discovered Ms. Svenson talking to herself. When she heard me, she turned around and stopped herself. She pulled out a handkerchief, blew her nose, and asked what I wanted.

"Is everything okay?" I said, concerned.

"Fine," was all she said. She blew her nose again and went into the kitchen, where she busied herself wiping up the counter.

That was odd, I thought. She had definitely not been herself for a while.

I got my drink of water, and as I was putting the glass in the sink, I noticed something peculiar. There was a set of hooks attached to the side of one of the china cabinets, from which hung numerous keys. One in particular caught my eye. Not wanting Svenson to catch on to what I was looking at, I casually made my way over to the hooks. I was close enough to make out that the attached metal tag on the single key said "Napa Public Storage #121."

That's strange. Why would anybody in this household need a public storage facility with the kind of space available here, unless they were hiding something they didn't want anyone else to know about? Like the wine! I hung out until Svenson left the kitchen, but just as I was about to make a move to swipe the key, she returned and foiled my plan. I hung out longer, pretending to listen to messages on my phone.

Once again, she left the room, and I made a move to lift the key. Again, she returned before I could do the deed. I hoped she would leave the kitchen yet again, so I could have another go at it, but she seemed destined to stay this time.

I decided to ask her about it.

"Do you know anything about this key?" I said, pointing at it.

"No," she said, taking my water glass and placing it in the dishwasher.

When she stepped out of the room again, I jotted down the name of the place and the unit number on a piece of paper I found on a pad attached to the side of the fridge.

When Rossi emerged into the hallway from being interrogated by Georgey, I asked him about it.

"I have no idea," he said.

I posed the same question to Lambeck when I ran into him a little later. He couldn't tell me. I caught McCall at one point and questioned him, but he just waved me off, shaking his head.

Well, somebody has to know something about it, I thought. The Keebler Elves didn't put it there. Somebody was lying.

I called Charlie and asked him to look into the storage place for me. "Get an address and opening hours," I said. "And get back to me pronto!"

"Will do, chief!"

As I started to go upstairs to use the washroom, the nearest one on the main level being occupied, I ran into Emily on her way down, accompanied by her private nurse. I hadn't seen her since we'd found her overdosed.

"Emily, how are you?" I said, touching her arm.

"Very tired," she said.

She looked it, too. Her eyes were glazed. Apparently, she was being kept sedated to keep her from doing anything stupid again. When I asked how she was holding up, she started to cry. The nurse told me that was enough chitchat—Emily had to be questioned by Georgey as well, and needed to maintain her strength. She hustled her off to the library.

From that, I guessed that Georgey was now through with the staff and into family members. I had wanted to ask Emily about the key, but couldn't. Besides, Emily was so out of it, I doubt whether she would have been any help anyway.

But when I returned downstairs, Denise emerged from the library.

"Do you know anything about that key to a unit in a public storage facility hanging on the side of the china cabinet in the kitchen?" I said.

"Don't know what you're talking about," she said.

Just then, my cell phone rang. It was Charlie. The storage facility was on Coombsville Road, on the outskirts of the town of Napa. They were open pretty much twenty-four seven. Charlie asked if I wanted rates. I told him no.

Before I left to check out the facility, I stepped out onto the patio off the kitchen to make a few calls. As this case had moved on and I had gotten more tied up in it, I had been neglecting my other business. My publisher had left several messages wanting to know how the new book was coming along. The editor of one of my regular columns was awaiting my feedback on his idea for a future piece. The college needed an answer as to whether I could cover another prof's class while he was away. In other words, other folks I was working for were starting to wonder why they hadn't heard from me.

After that, as I began to leave the house, I found that Georgey, too, was wrapping things up.

"So, any leads?" I said once outside, leaning on my car.

"I hope you appreciate what I'm doing for you by not coming down on that phony Lambeck yet," he said.

I put my arm around his shoulder and told him there was a 1997 Brunello with his name on it in my wine cellar. Besides, it would only be a few more days.

"You're not trying to bribe a police officer, are you?" he said, his hands on his hips.

I left that alone and asked about the most probable suspects, especially with regard to brown hair and left-handedness.

"Everyone with both criteria, either at the auction house or here at the estate, had an alibi," Georgey said. "I haven't had a chance yet to question Patricia and Horace Botner, but they were indisposed and at the hospital at the time of Philips's death. I will question Wader and the Spezzos when back in San Fran." And since he was getting nowhere with the hair/left-handed approach, he said his next step would be to take hair samples from all the suspects to see if they matched the DNA of the hair found at the crime scene.

Georgey took off for San Francisco, and I proceeded to Napa Public Storage.

En route, I thought about Patricia. I had not seen her since Johnny Spezzo's funeral, and she looked terrible there. I called to check in. She sounded so exhausted, and still painfully upset. I asked how Horace was doing, and she told me he was still in a coma. He had been beaten really badly, and his prognosis, especially at his age, didn't look good. She started to cry, telling me she didn't know what she was going to do. I offered to help in some way, but she refused. When I hung up, I felt terrible for her.

I found the storage facility without too much difficulty and drove in through the gates. Although surrounded by greenery, the facility itself looked as if many trees had been removed to make room for it. There were numerous gray-and-white storage units, all linked together like row houses, some larger and some smaller. Just inside the gate was the office. I stepped inside.

"I'm looking to rent a unit," I said, gazing around the office.

"Yes, sir," said the man at the counter. "What size?"

"Something small," I said.

He showed me a schematic of the facility, pointing out the small ones available. None was near number 121.

"Follow me, please."

I followed him outside and around to unit number eighteen. He opened it for a look-see, but what was there to look at? It was a six-by-six-foot square box with a cement floor and a sliding metal door. Nothing unusual!

"Well?" the guy said.

I asked if he could give me a couple minutes alone to think about it. He looked at me funny, probably wondering why anyone needed to think about something like that, but agreed. "Come see me when you're done," he said.

Once the guy was out of sight, I quickly ran around, looking for number 121. I found it about two rows over, down at the other end, not too far from the front gate. It was also a small unit. I tried the lock, but it was secure.

How was I going to find out who it belonged to? I racked my brain. Then—an idea!

I looked around for something I could use to jimmy the door. I didn't want to break in, you understand—I simply wanted to make it look as if someone had tried, causing the guy from the office to contact its owner and ask him to come out to make sure everything within was secure.

I found a sizable rock and worked it between the bottom runner of the sliding metal door just enough so it got wedged in there, causing that part of the door to remain ajar. I tried peeking in, but the opening was so low to the ground that I would have to have my eyeball in the dirt to see anything. And even if I could, it was way too dark in there to get a proper look.

Then I headed back to the office and told the guy that, during a stroll around the facility, I had discovered an attempted break-in. I led him to number 121.

"I'd better notify the owners immediately," he said after checking it out, hustling back to the office.

As he dashed off, he yelled back, asking if I wanted to rent the unit he had showed me.

"Not after this!" I said.

I went back out the gate in my car, parked up a secluded driveway, grabbed the pair of binoculars, and moved by foot alongside the road past the entrance. I waited.

About a half hour passed—and then, some activity. I heard a car pull up into the facility. I could hear voices—men's voices. All of a sudden, there was the guy from the office, standing with two people right in front of number 121.

It was Lambeck and Amos—together. For some reason, they looked a little confused.

That's when I was spotted, chased, and beaten in front of my home.

Hopefully, you remember.

CHAPTER 29

I woke up in California Pacific Medical Center with contusions, cuts, a couple of fractured ribs, and a slight concussion. I had a huge shiner, a split fat lip, a cut on my beezer, and a swollen cheekbone, and my forehead was blue. Around both my eyes were dried, bloodied gashes. I wasn't a pretty sight.

The doctor told me it was a good thing I was in decent physical shape, or I'd have been a lot worse off. If Charlie hadn't come along about 10 p.m. to ask if I wanted to go over to the Gull for a nightcap, I might not even have made it to the hospital.

"You just get some rest," I heard the nurse telling me, "and I'll be back later to look in on you. If you need anything at all, just ring that buzzer there. Okay?"

"Thanks," I said.

With that, she left me alone with my thoughts. I was somewhat groggy, probably from painkillers.

Not really aware of how much time had passed, I saw the door swing open, and in walked an orderly. He was a big guy with curly hair and a mustache, dressed in scrubs. I paid no attention to him. Why would I? It was a hospital, and orderlies were all over the place. But if I hadn't been so sedated, I might have known what was coming.

The guy approached the bed, saying nothing. When he reached into his pants pocket, I expected him to pull out a stethoscope, thermometer, or some other medical paraphernalia. Instead, he pulled out a switchblade.

The sound of the blade extending rang in my ears. I stared at him in disbelief.

"What the hell are you doing?" I said, completely shocked and dazed, and starting to panic.

"Finishing the job," he said.

In what seemed like slow motion, he raised the knife above my head, preparing to thrust it forward. When I stared into his cold, dark eyes, there was no emotion whatsoever. It was as if he was going to do some benign, meaningless thing like flick away a dust bunny, not snuff out someone's life. I was absolutely terrified.

And I finally recognized him. It was one of the thugs from the back-room of the Italian restaurant.

I cried out and, with all my strength, pounded at the buzzer.

Just as the knife began its downward motion, Georgey came running into the room and grabbed the guy's arm from behind, stopping the plunging knife from making contact. They staggered backwards together, struggling for the knife. The guy was strong, and managed to catch Georgey on the hand, cutting him. I screamed for help and continued to pound on the buzzer.

Suddenly, two officers ran into the room, apprehended and cuffed the assailant, and escorted him out.

Georgey was panting like a wolfhound.

"You okay?" he said, trying to catch his breath.

"Scared friggin' silly," I said, my head spinning. "You?"

He told me he was fine as he took a towel from the bathroom and wrapped it around his bleeding hand.

"It's a damn good thing I came along when I did, or else you'd be a pincushion," he said. "Did you recognize the guy?"

"I think he's one of the guys I saw at that Italian restaurant with Lambeck," I said. "He may also be one of the guys who chased me back from Napa."

I was still shaking and dozy, and couldn't be totally sure about the accuracy of my last statement.

"Whoa, slow down," said Georgey. "What Italian restaurant?"

I realized I hadn't told Georgey about that. When I did, he was furious.

"You're not a cop, you idiot! You could have gotten yourself killed!" he yelled.

But I was petrified enough at the moment and didn't need him chewing me out. Georgey took a few minutes, got a hold of himself, and said he was placing a uniformed officer outside my room until all this was over. Making some comment about having a doctor look at his cut hand, he told me to get some rest and said he'd check on me later. With that, the detective was gone. I didn't tell him about Lambeck, Amos, and the storage facility.

I lay there, confused, scared, and less groggy. I guess this episode had shocked some of the sedation out of me. I wondered what on earth might happen next. This case had become far more than I had bargained for.

Suddenly, there was a knock at the door. *Oh crap, what now?* I braced myself and apprehensively said, "Come in."

It was Sadie and Julia. I breathed a sigh of relief.

Sadie came hobbling over, threw her arms around me, and gave me a huge hug and kiss.

"My poor baby," she said. "Are you okay? I was so worried about you." She didn't cry, but there were tears in her eyes.

I assured her that I was fine—still shaking, but fine! When she took a step back and looked at me, I could tell she disagreed.

I stared at Julia. She looked at me with great concern, shook her head from side to side, and smiled. Coming forward, she gently touched my face, and all my cuts and bruises. Bending over, she gave me a tender kiss. It was like being caressed by an angel.

"Oh, Woody," was all she said. I reached out and cuddled her the best I could.

At that moment, nothing else needed to be said. They both sat on the edge of my bed, one on either side, and we huddled together in silence.

After they left, the doctor came in, examined my chart, and said I could go home the next day.

Finally left alone, and somewhat secure in my safety, I started to go over in my mind what I had seen at the storage facility before being followed and beaten. My plan to find out who occupied the unit had worked. I hadn't been sure who to expect. All my theories involved more than one person, and both Lambeck and Amos were definitely suspects high on my list, but *not* together. That they looked a little confused bothered me. The worst thing about all of this was that I still didn't know if the wine was in that storage unit.

The next day, I was released from the hospital. It was interesting to note that nobody from the McCall family, his staff, or his friends even called or dropped by while I was there. That in itself was somewhat suspicious.

I had been told to take it easy at home for a few days, so I worked out of my office. A police officer stood guard outside my front door in case anybody wanted to deliver an encore performance. His name was Bill Clark, a nice, well-built chap about my age, with dark hair, a mustache, and an easygoing personality.

Charlie came by to help out with whatever I wanted him to do. Julia continued to stay with Sadie, and a police officer guarded them as well. I spent the day mulling over the evidence I had accumulated. Georgey called me often to update me on his investigation. He told me that the DNA testing was unsuccessful.

I had completely forgotten about McCall's ultimatum when, on the second day out of the hospital, he called. Not even asking how I was doing, he simply told me I was done and to send him an invoice. He would pay me what he owed me.

I was really ticked. I had put so much time and effort into this case, and I had almost gotten killed in the process, and he was dismissing me without so much as a "thank you."

"That's not fair!" I said, raising my voice.

"You've got nothing," he said, quite bluntly.

That was partly true. I had uncovered certain things, but I still didn't know for sure who stole the wine, or even where it was exactly.

"Give me a little more time?" I said.

More than a very large part of me wanted so badly to walk away from this case and tell McCall to stick it. I couldn't stand him. I'd almost gotten killed. However, I really needed to do this for Sadie's sake. Solve the mystery, obtain the money, and get Sadie that operation!

"No. I've already hired someone else."

That really pissed me off. Without thinking, I blurted something out: "I know who stole your wine."

The silence at the other end of the phone was tense as he processed what I had said. In that timeframe, I thought, *What the hell are you saying?* I couldn't believe the words had come out of my mouth. I started to sweat.

"What?" he finally said, sounding absolutely astonished.

"You heard me."

"I don't believe you," he said with a snarky tone.

Oh, now he's calling me a liar. That enraged me even more.

"Well, I guess you'll never find out, because you just fired me."

That angered him.

"Look, Robins, I've put up with your unorthodox approach to investigating, your stupid questions, your hanging about all the time, and your cornball clothes," McCall said. "If you know who stole my wine, you had better tell me."

His threatening attitude really put me off.

"All right," I said, calming myself down, "but it'll cost you."

"You're bribing me now? I told you to send me an invoice and I would pay you for the time invested."

"It's not money I want, but respect," I said. "You start calling me *Mr. Robins.*"

I was fuming. Ever since I had started this case, he had talked down to me, bullied me, and treated me like I was inept. I was sick of it.

"You're nuts," he said, starting to laugh.

"Do you want your wine back or not?" I said, quite smugly.

His laughing stopped.

"You're bluffing," he said, sounding downright sure of himself. "You don't have any idea who stole it."

"Can you afford to take that chance?"

There were several long moments of silence until he spoke.

"Okay, *Mr. Robins,* let's hear what you have to say."

"You gather all your staff, family, and friends that are part of this case together at your place," I said. "Tell them it's a meeting, party, whatever. I don't give a damn what excuse you use, just so long as they're all together at the same time. *Do not* tell them I will be there. That's when I will unveil your thief."

He thought about it a moment.

"Monday night at 8 p.m.!" He hung up.

I sat there stupefied. *What have I done?* I had gotten so caught up in the guy's dismissive attitude and disrespect that I had promised something I couldn't deliver—at least not at this point. What to do now?

It was Saturday. I had forty-eight hours to somehow pull this together. If only I had my tape recorder. I prayed it would miraculously turn up. Searching the house and car thoroughly again later on Saturday and on Sunday morning brought no results, so I gave up all hope of finding it. I also spent this time trying to work out how I was going to play Monday evening.

That night, I tossed and turned, trying to come up with an answer, but it escaped me. Monday, about mid-morning, I contemplated calling McCall, swallowing my pride, and telling him I was wrong. Several times, I had the phone in my hand and was about to dial his number, but then stopped myself. If I went through with this and fell flat on my face, which it looked as if I was going to do, I would be the world's biggest fool. Was I willing to take that chance?

I guess I was, because at about 6 p.m., I donned a pair of black, pleated, cotton slacks, a solid, light blue linen dress shirt, a double-breasted, light gray worsted wool sports jacket, and black loafers. Adorning my wavy brown locks was a smoky gray homburg.

I figured I'd play it by ear. I had a couple of far-out ideas I might present and a few psychological maneuvers that might make the suspects incriminate themselves. Beyond that, I was driving at night without any headlights.

I called Georgey and told him what I was up to.

"Are you sure that's a smart idea?" he said, concerned.

At that point, I wasn't sure of anything, but I needed to do something drastic. If this little drama of mine didn't call for drastic action, then I didn't know what did! Besides, I had my pride at stake. Maybe even my reputation! And especially Aunt Sadie's wellbeing.

I told Georgey to meet me at McCall's at about 9 p.m., but not to come into the house or barge in while I was doing my thing. If and when I needed him, I'd signal through the living room window by waving him in. He'd just be there ready with several officers should the situation arise.

I was damn nervous. Aside from having no idea what was going to happen, it would be the first time I'd been out of the house since leaving the hospital. Officer Clark, who had been guarding my house, accompanied me. He, too, would wait outside with Georgey.

CHAPTER 30

The drive up to Napa was uneventful, and we arrived about quarter past eight. I could see by the number of cars at the estate that probably all who needed to be there were there. Officer Clark waited outside, and would hook up with Georgey when he made the scene.

I went into the house without knocking, carrying a small bag of select items I thought might come in handy. Everyone was in the living room, sipping drinks.

When I stepped into the room, conversation came to an abrupt stop, and all eyes focused on me, surprise across everyone's face.

Sure enough, everyone was there—even folks who normally didn't come into the house. Amos in his chauffeur's uniform looked very uncomfortable. Rodrigo, dressed in a pair of khakis and a beige-colored shirt, sat in an easy chair, tossing and turning like a fish on dry land. Rossi, in his civies, leaned against the mantelpiece. Ms. Svenson, clad in a pantsuit, lounged on one of the couches, looking stern and unhappy. Lambeck, in his usual garb, occupied the other end of another couch. The Waders and Spezzos, in business attire, stood by the patio doors. Denise, looking great in a navy blue dress, was at the other side of the room, far away from Amos, and from Emily, who wore dark slacks and a blouse as she curled up in another lounger. She looked out of it, and her nurse sat nearby. Patricia, still looking as if she had been put through the ringer, stood with her hands in her pockets, staring out the window. She was alone—Horace was still in the hospital. The boss, with arms folded, stood like a statue in the doorway.

A silence hung in the air like a bad smell.

McCall started to say a few words: "Robins here thinks ..." He stopped as he saw me glaring at him intensely. "*Mr. Robins* thinks he knows who stole my wine," he said, "and he's going to tell us." He rolled his eyes and almost chuckled at the end of his statement.

Every eye was plastered on me. I was the main attraction, the star, and I was bloody nervous. My heart was pounding in my chest, my palms were sweaty, and I felt a bit nauseated. I had never done this before.

I took a deep breath.

"First of all, I'd like to thank everyone for their cooperation during my investigation," I said. "It was much appreciated."

My voice trembled a bit at first, but eventually stabilized.

"This case has been very difficult and puzzling and gathering clues has not been an easy task. The evidence is—"

"Get on with it. We haven't got all night," McCall said.

I suppose I was trying to buy some time by pontificating a bit, but McCall wasn't going for it. I gave him a dirty look and turned my attention to the Waders.

"I have no beef with you at all, sir," I said to Ralph. "You have been most helpful."

Turning next to the Spezzos, I basically reiterated my comment—with one exception: "I do, however, have some misgivings about your son."

"My son?" Sam said, glaring at me. "What do you mean?"

"His expertise in computer surveillance in the Army made him the perfect person to sabotage the vault's security system. He was a computer whiz kid. If anyone could do it—"

"Who the hell do you think you're talking about?" Sam said. "Johnny was a good boy. Have some respect for the dead."

"I'm truly sorry for his passing, Mr. Spezzo, and understand how hard it must be for you and your family," I said, "but the fact remains, of all the suspects, he was best equipped to get into that vault. And with the help of his old Army buddy, Joey Touchstone, whose company he recommended to create and install the system, the finger points directly at him."

"That's plain ridiculous," Sam said, sounding agitated.

"The big question is why. You folks are well-off, so money couldn't have been an issue."

I turned my attention to Emily, who looked as if she was in another world.

"From what I understand, Emily, you blamed your father for your mother's death—for not acting fast enough to get her medical help. You hated him for it. You said he loved his damn wine more than his wife. Therefore, you convinced your computer whiz-kid boyfriend to help steal his prized possession, that Burgundy, just to spite him."

"What?" Emily said, with a glazed look in her eyes.

I walked over to her and repeated what I had said. She still looked at me funny. "Do you understand what I'm saying, Emily?"

Finally, she seemed to comprehend and became somewhat more lucid.

"That's not true," she finally said, as tears began to run down her face. "Yes, I hated him, but I didn't steal his wine." Emily looked groggily at her father. She was having trouble focusing.

McCall's face turned ghostly white, his mouth fell open, and he stared at his daughter in disbelief.

"I didn't talk my Johnny into anything," she said, trying to get up, but she fell back into her seat. "I loved him, and I almost betrayed him with my feelings for you. I hate myself. I don't deserve to live." She started to bawl heavily. The nurse went to her side to comfort her.

Although I knew she had feelings for me, especially from her behavior at McCall's party, I was surprised to hear her publicly admit it—and I could now see that, in light of Johnny's death, her guilt was most certainly a contributing factor in her attempted suicide.

"You, Johnny, and Touchstone were prime suspects, all conspiring to steal the wine—not for resale, but simply to separate it from Mr. McCall," I said. "A lot of evidence weighed heavily in favor of that theory. However, the fact that someone was trying to sell the wine put something of a kibosh to it."

I went over to where Emily was sitting and lifted her face up with my hand to look into her eyes.

"There was something in your eyes, Emily, when you spoke about helping people, as you did at the drop-in centers. It was a sincerity, an honesty, even an innocence, that made me think you were telling the truth."

The eyes speak volumes, and I didn't really think she was capable of the theft. I was merely trying to get a reaction from Emily and the Spezzos to see what happened.

Then I turned to Rodrigo, the gardener.

"Mr. Rodrigo, I admire your bravery in leaving your home country to come to a new one and especially your determination to use the money you're making to go to school for viticulture. You said you knew nothing about French wine, and I believed your story about not having a chance to look at your poster on how to read a French wine label. Beyond that, I couldn't find any evidence against you."

This seemed to please him, and he relaxed a little more.

Next, I focused on Rossi, the chef.

"I love your cooking, Roberto, and I thank you for your hospitality during my time at the house. The fact that you assumed the wine cellar door was opened with a key was indeed just that—an assumption. I have nothing else on you."

Then I turned my gaze to Amos.

"Poor Mr. Amos!" I said. "Most people judge you by what you look like and automatically assume you're a *bad boy*."

That certainly seemed to be what Emily got, and I was sure others did too. Not surprisingly, he did absolutely nothing to dispel that image.

"However, for a guy who thinks 'wine is for sissies,' you had a few wine corks in your ashtray in the garage. You also contradicted yourself at the Devil's Lair, holding a glass of wine while shooting pool."

"How the hell do you know that?" he said, starting to get hot under the collar.

I ignored his question.

"Not all of everyone's suspicions of you are unjustified. You were indeed involved with something underhanded as you waited at that club for a deal to break."

"You bastard! You've been spying on me," Amos said.

I had to tread carefully here. I didn't want to infuriate the beast and have him go berserk on me.

"Yes—it is most unfortunate that people don't see the real Mr. Amos. You sure shocked me with your interest in classical music," I said.

There was a hush in the room.

"However," I said, "one person does know the real you."

When I looked over in Denise's direction, she just looked back at me coldly, then scanned the room.

"Isn't that right, Denise?" I said, staring directly at her.

"You don't know what you're talking about," she said, shifting on her feet. She did a great job of playing it cool.

"Oh, come now, my dear. You've been sneaking and playing around with Amos for a while now, right under your father's nose," I said.

There was a gasp among the other attendees, and McCall's mouth fell open even further.

"You're nuts," Denise said, holding her ground. Her face was slightly flushed and beads of perspiration formed on her brow.

"You'd meet him often at his place in Rutherford and head over to that bar."

"Drop dead," she said, looking away.

McCall's face turned four more shades of red as he looked back and forth from her to Amos.

"That's where you two met up with your comrade in crime to work out the details of the heist. Then, you alone met with the same guy to make the exchange."

"You're out of your friggin' mind," she said, smirking to herself. "Besides, you can't prove anything."

"What if I told you I have it all on video?" I lied.

Her demeanor immediately changed. Now she looked worried.

"You're lying," she said, looking back at Amos.

"Am I?" I said.

"Is this true, Denise?" McCall said.

"Not at all," Denise said.

"You'd steal from your own father?" McCall said, tapping himself on the chest.

"No, I didn't take your stupid wine!"

"And you've been seeing my chauffeur behind my back? After all I've done for you? How could you? Let me see that video," he demanded, coming toward me, hand out to receive it.

I started for the bag I had brought in to retrieve a DVD that didn't exist.

"All right, it's true!" Denise said, staring directly at her father. "I have been seeing him, but it's not just a fling. I love him."

With that, she raced over to Amos, putting her arm around him as she stared defiantly back at her father.

The gesture was all I had needed. *Thank God!*

Everyone looked shocked. McCall was beside himself, and started toward the couple. I hoped he wouldn't get violent. Patricia stepped in and pulled McCall aside.

"With my damn chauffeur! My damn chauffeur," he kept repeating, shaking his head.

It was then I realized why Amos was concerned that Emily didn't like him and might be trying to get him fired. Perhaps he thought she knew about his affair with Denise and would tell McCall. It *would* be a way to get back at her sister.

"Two questions, then," I said to Denise and Amos. "What did you do with the wine, and why steal it?"

"We don't know anything about that damn wine," Amos said, Denise's arm still around him.

"Don't you?"

Getting out of Denise's grasp, he stepped toward me. I scooted behind Ralph Wader for protection, thinking he was going to attack.

"Those corks in the ashtray in the garage, I know nothing about," said Amos. "The wine in the bar, I was holding for Denise while she was in the can."

"But when she came out of the washroom, you still had it in your hand," I said.

"I hadn't given it back to her yet because we were talking to some hippy at the bar." He stopped himself, cocked his head to one side, and stared at me intently. "Wait a minute. That was you . . . in disguise," he said, as the realization kicked in. "Son of a bitch! I knew there was something fishy about him!" He came at me again. Once more I nipped behind Wader for protection. I wasn't sure I believed him about the wine.

"What about the deal that went down?" I said, staring at him from behind the lawyer.

"Not that it's any of your friggin' business, but I managed to sell, on the black market, a rare, limited-edition boxed set of *The Rubenstein Collection*. Classical music! I was working, so Denise did the transaction. That's the deal, you ass."

The room was filled with silence. Amos returned to Denise, and they both scowled at me. I heard what sounded like cars pulling up outside and assumed Georgey and some officers had arrived. Going over and peering out a window, I found I was right.

Well, that didn't pan out, I thought. *Let's try another approach.*

CHAPTER 31

D one with Amos for now, I turned my attention to Lambeck. The whole time I was grilling Amos and Denise, he had just sat there, looking bored.

"So, Mr. Lambeck, you grew up in London's West End, did you?" I said, walking over in his direction.

He concurred.

"And you'd say you know the West End quite well?"

"Like the back of my hand," he said.

"Then you'd know that little pub called the Vicar's Nose on Hanbury Street off Brick Lane?" I said.

"Certainly do, sir."

"Well, that's interesting, Mr. Lambeck," I said. "Hanbury Street is in the East End, and there is no such place as the Vicar's Nose."

He turned beet red and looked around at the others.

"Let's be honest here, Mr. Lambeck," I said. "If you're English, then I'm Ethel Merman. That phony British accent of yours may have fooled some folks, but not me. And the club in New York you say you worked at previously: What was it called?"

I searched my somewhat lousy memory for the name, but he provided it: "The Empire Club," he said, his voice shaking.

"Yes, the Empire Club! Well, they've never heard of you."

I hadn't checked that out. I was just trying to get a reaction out of him. He started to sweat.

"You're quite mistaken, sir," he said, his fingers nervously tapping on the end table.

"You actually are from New York, though. Is that where you studied acting?"

"What the hell are you talking about?" he said, looking at me oddly, starting to get mad.

"Well, is it, Mr. Lambeck?" I said.

No answer! He shifted nervously in his seat.

"Come on, Michael—or should I say Mickey 'Mitch' Lambini?" I said, pointing my finger at him.

That did it.

"I'll kill you!" he said, getting up and coming at me with his fist in the air.

I immediately moved backwards, ready to protect myself, when Amos stepped forward, pushing Lambeck back into his seat.

"You make a move and I'll snap you like a twig," Amos said, staring at him.

Shaking, I half-expected Lambeck to pull out a gun. Considering who he was, I was actually surprised I hadn't found one in his room when I searched it the second time.

"So why did you steal the wine?" I said, gaining my composure and continuing on.

"I didn't," said Lambeck.

"Sure you did. You and your hoodlum buddies there from the Veronese family were going to sell it and split the money."

"You're absolutely out of your mind," he said.

"Yeah, and 'Little Larry' Dentico and Dominick 'Quiet Dom' Cirillo were just in town on vacation, eh?"

Again, he got up and came at me. Once more, Amos pushed him back onto the couch, telling him not to move. My heart was pounding in my chest.

With this new information, McCall was not looking well. He was red as a tomato and sweating profusely, looking as if he was going to have a heart attack. He slowly went over to the liquor cabinet, poured himself a large scotch, and downed it in one gulp.

"So you had nothing to do with the theft of the wine?" I said, crossing my arms.

"Not a thing!" He started tapping his feet nervously and looked away, his left eyebrow twitching.

"Then why'd you have those goons chase me back to my house and beat me up?"

"You're crazy, and I don't have a clue what you're talking about," he said.

"Don't lie to me. It was the same two thugs who you were hanging out with in the backroom of that restaurant in Vallejo," I said.

"Damn you!" he screamed. "I'm gonna break your neck!"

The crowd in the room gasped, and whispers were heard all around—not because he once again got up and came at me, but because, with this outburst, his British accent was suddenly and completely gone, and in its place, his New York accent.

Amos again pushed him back into his seat.

"One more time and I'll break your legs, Lambeck," Amos said, glaring at him. "Or should I say, Lambini."

I don't mind telling you, by this point, I was scared silly, but I held my ground.

"And I suppose you and your buddies had nothing to do with the beating of Horace Botner?" I said.

Suddenly, Patricia, who had gone back to staring out a side window after securing McCall, came to life and turned around.

"I had nothing to do with that," Lambeck said, shaking his head.

"You and Horace were poker buddies. Did you guys not play cards with your hoodlum comrades? Did Horace not lose a bundle to them?" I said. "He couldn't pay up, so that's why he was beaten!"

"You're nuts."

All of a sudden, from across the room, Patricia cried out and headed for Lambeck. Hurling herself at him, she started punching away and screaming, "I'll kill you! I'll kill you! I'll kill you!"

"Get her the hell off of me!" Lambeck yelled.

Denise and Sam Spezzo raced forward and pulled Patricia off him. Denise held her in her arms while she sobbed.

There were a few moments of silence, except for Patricia's crying, before I took a deep breath and continued on.

"So, Mr. Lambeck, you would have us believe that you had nothing to do with the theft of the wine and know nothing about Horace's beating—or whether Horace himself tried to steal the wine to sell so he could pay your mob buddies back. You also know nothing about why I was chased and beaten?" I said.

"That's right."

I half-expected to get a reaction from Patricia with that comment about Horace, but she said nothing.

"And the line about hearing footsteps on the stairs going down to the basement the night the wine went missing—which nobody else heard—

and all that about Ms. Svenson spending so much time down there was all garbage?"

"Well, she does spend a lot of time down in the basement," Lambeck said.

"So, if you had nothing to do with the theft of the wine, why did you show up at Napa Storage Facility?"

"I was simply sent to pick up something," he said. "I wasn't told what. I was just doing my job."

"Why was Mr. Amos with you?"

"He drove me," he said.

"Is that true, Mr. Amos?"

He agreed.

"So neither of you knew why you were going to that storage facility or what you were supposed to pick up?" I said, somewhat perplexed. "Did that not strike you as odd?"

They both looked at each other and nodded.

Thinking about it, they *had* looked rather confused when I spied on them at the unit through my binoculars.

"And what exactly did you pick up?" I said, leaning in.

Everyone's ears perked up.

They both said there was nothing.

"Nothing?"

They repeated their answer.

"And what was in the storage unit?" I said, leaning in even further.

Again, they both said there was nothing. No wonder they looked so confused.

I finally asked who sent them on this mission.

"Ms. Svenson!" Amos said.

"After the trip out to the storage facility, did you ask her why there was nothing to pick up?"

"Of course we did," Lambeck said. "We're not stupid."

"So what did she say?"

"She claimed it was a mistake," said Amos.

"A mistake! Did you not find that strange?"

"Sure we did," said Lambeck, "but Ms. Svenson had been acting quite strange as of late, and we simply wrote it off to that."

So I turned my attention to Ms. Svenson.

CHAPTER 32

"**M**s. Svenson, are you in the habit of sending people on wild goose chases?" I said.

She didn't respond. I went over to the coffee table, where there were some glasses and a pitcher of water and poured myself some. Taking a sip, I continued on.

"So, Ms. Svenson, you seem to run a tight ship here. You keep everything in this household going smoothly, don't you? You're a jack-of-all-trades, according to Mr. McCall—pretty good with plumbing, electrical, and mechanical, and you're even a sommelier. I believe the expression he used was 'better than most men.'"

She just nodded.

"You've been with him now over two decades," I said. "You knew his wife. You watched his girls grow up. You're like a member of the family."

Again, she nodded.

"You're the only one other than Mr. McCall who handles the wine, although he is the sole controller of the vault. Correct?" I said.

This time, she spoke: "Yes."

"And you were obviously tied up all evening serving dinner when the wine was stolen."

I took a step back, waited a minute, then put my glass down on a side table.

"Ladies and gentlemen," I said, "most of you will be surprised to learn that the wine was not stolen the night of the dinner party, but previously."

A hush fell over the room. I looked around to see the reactions. Confusion danced across many faces.

Here's where I really started to fly by the seat of my pants.

"The wine was removed from the vault at an earlier date, and exited the house via a secret passageway."

There was a gasp among the crowd.

"But the monitor of the vault still displayed the wine there the night of the dinner," said Ralph Wader. "How is that possible?"

"That's a good question, sir, and it could easily be done by veiling or masking," I said. "However, this system was not set up for it, and it couldn't be implemented after its creation. Not even a computer whiz kid like Johnny Spezzo could pull that off. To be honest, that issue had puzzled me as well, and I had been searching for all the complex solutions to this problem when the answer was actually right under my nose.

"When I met Johnny at dinner the first night with Mr. McCall, he helped him sort out a computer issue—a frozen screen. He said a nasty virus could do this. Even my computer guy, when he was out at my office, informed me of such a virus. This is what happened with the vault's monitor," I said.

"Wait a minute," Ralph said, looking very puzzled. "Do you mean to say that a screen-freezing virus just happened to conveniently and coincidentally attack the security system computer right before the wine was going to be stolen?"

"That does sound rather ridiculous, implausible, and far-fetched, doesn't it?" I said. "What I'm saying is that someone introduced it into the system in order to freeze it up, so the image of the wine permanently remained while it was still there *and* after it was actually lifted."

"Wouldn't James have noticed it?"

"Why would he? The screen showed the wine in the vault. What else did he need to know? He said himself that he hadn't actually gone into the vault for a few weeks. The big questions are: Who did it, and when was it done?" I said.

Now I was going to go out on a limb big-time. My palms began to sweat and my heartbeat picked up. Up to this point, I still didn't know who stole the wine, but I was hoping my little prank here would reveal the culprit.

"About a week ago, I took the liberty of putting some indelible ink on the door to the secret passageway," I said. "It's colorless and odorless, and undetectable, and it stays wet for a long time. It will stain the hands of anyone who comes in contact with it, and the stain will linger about ten days."

I wasn't even sure if there was such a product on the market, but I watched every person in that room carefully to see who would look at their hands. Only the guilty party would be concerned that their hands were stained. But as I scanned the room, nobody made a move to examine their hands. They simply stared back at me and looked at others for a reaction. *That's strange*, I thought. *Could I be wrong?* I started to get nervous. *Time to pull out the secret weapon!*

"What I neglected to tell you is that the stains are undetectable to the naked eye, but can be seen under a black light. Then, it shows as green. I took the liberty of bringing a black light along."

Reaching into the small bag I had brought along, I pulled out a long, fluorescent black light and looked for a place to plug it in. Finding an outlet to my right on the wall, I plugged it in and turned it on. The room was suddenly bathed in a surreal luminescence. Teeth and anything white came to life.

"All right, everyone, put down your drinks, take your hands out of your pockets, and hold them up, palms out," I said.

One by one, each attendee relieved their hands of anything they were holding, took them out of their pockets, and held them up for me to examine—everyone, that is, except one person.

"Are you not going to show me your hands, Ms. Svenson?" I said, moving toward her.

All eyes were on her.

"Come now. Don't be shy."

She looked nervous, and slowly removed her hands from her pockets and held them out, almost afraid to gaze at them. But there was nothing—not a mark. She heaved a sigh of relief so big it could have floated the Queen Mary.

Staring at her, I said, "How interesting! There was no ink. I lied."

Another gasp filled the room. Believe me, I was as shocked as everyone else that Svenson was the one who held back. I couldn't believe my little prank had worked.

McCall, looking completely perplexed, just stared at her and shook his head. He looked like a man who had just lost his very best friend.

"So, Ms. Svenson, it would appear you gave yourself away," I said, turning off the black light, unplugging it, and returning it to my bag.

She said absolutely nothing, but Sam Spezzo went over and held her as if apprehending a criminal.

"You certainly had all of us fooled," I said.

CHAPTER 33

"Let me see if I can piece this all together," I said, walking over to an empty spot on one of the couches and sitting down.

"Sometime before the dinner party, Ms. Svenson, you got into the vault. How? When I examined the computer keyboard of the vault the first day I arrived, I noticed small remnants of baby powder. You had delicately sprinkled a little on the keyboard once before Mr. McCall had gone into the vault, and could then see what keys had been pushed to open it. He obviously hadn't noticed that himself. Although whoever had come out from the security company to check out the vault had touched the keyboard, some powder still remained. I found an open container of baby powder in your room when I searched it. I thought nothing of it at the time. Many people use baby powder to prevent chafing and other things. Only just now, when you gave yourself away, did it click."

Svenson just looked at me.

"How you got the wine out of the house is another story. Mr. Amos had mentioned something about occasional blackouts. That's why he kept candles and a lantern in the garage. But according to the Northern California Power Agency, there were several blackouts about a week before the dinner party. You may have utilized one of these to make your theft easier. Won't you clarify this for us, Ms. Svenson?" I said, looking in her direction.

She gave no answer.

"I'm not surprised that you knew of the tunnel, Ms. Svenson," I said. "According to Mr. Wader, you were on the scene when this house was built, and you coordinated much of the work. He said there was a set of blueprints at the house here, but Mr. McCall was not aware of it. I'd bet, if we searched your room more thoroughly, we'd come up with those blueprints," I said. "Not that the new blueprints alone would indicate the secret passageway! You'd have to do as I did, and compare them with the schematics of the original dwelling at the Napa historical archives section of the public library—or know first-hand about the existing tunnels before, as you did."

Svenson, with no expression on her face, just stood there in Sam's grip.

"I noticed footprints in the mud along the bank under the stone bridge near the cottage the night Emily and I went for a stroll after dinner. They seemed like they were made by a woman's shoe, and I noticed mud on your shoes at one point later on. I must admit I had my suspicions about you, but for the life of me, I couldn't figure out any motivation. Oh, you were very cunning, stashing wine corks in Mr. Amos's ashtray in the garage and telling me you didn't trust Mr. Lambeck, just to make me think they were guilty."

She just stared at me.

"And that key to the storage facility! When I was recuperating in the hospital, the more I thought about it, the more it didn't make sense. Why would somebody leave a key to a secret storage place where they were stashing a stolen item so readily available and easy to find—unless they wanted me to! You meant for me to find it, but didn't allow me enough time alone to lift it. However, you knew I would note the info and check it out."

"But why would she lead you directly to where the wine was hidden?" Sam Spezzo said, a puzzled look on his face.

"Why indeed? The truth of the matter is the wine wasn't stashed in that storage unit at all. It never was," I said, redirecting my attention to Svenson. "You saw I was getting too close to an answer, so you created this decoy just to steer me off the track. And when Mr. Lambeck and Mr. Amos called and told you I had seen them there, you got some thugs to put a hit on me to scare me off the case once and for all, since threatening notes and tire-slashing didn't do it—nor attacking my girlfriend.

"Speaking of thugs, Ms. Svenson," I said, "you don't strike me as the kind of person who would know where to find guys like that. It's not like one can simply look "thugs" up in the Yellow Pages and call them. My guess is that you had to go through somebody else—somebody who actually had connections."

At this point, there was a tangible buzz in the room.

"Someone like Mr. Lambeck here," I said, moving in his direction and tapping him on the shoulder.

He turned and gave me a look so evil, it made my blood freeze and forced me to jump back.

"But you two despise each other, so he wasn't likely to do you any favors—that is, unless you had something on him that you could use to blackmail him into helping."

Svenson continued to play it as cool as a cucumber.

"Somehow, you found out that Mr. Lambeck was a phony, and you threatened to tell Mr. McCall unless he agreed to find you some thugs. How convenient that some of Mr. Lambeck's cohorts were in town and readily available! Isn't that true?" I said, staring at Lambeck.

He simply ignored me.

"So that's how you came to acquire the services of those mean dudes who followed me and beat me up," I said, turning back to Svenson. "Still, the most baffling part about all of this is why. Why would you steal a wine from an employer who, by all accounts, has been kind, paid you well, put you up, and basically treated you like family for over two decades? It doesn't make any sense."

But now, certain questionable things I had noted earlier seemed to fall into place. I attempted to put them into perspective.

"Ms. Svenson, I couldn't help but notice that you often stare at Mr. McCall. I must admit I find that odd," I said. "When I snooped around in your room one day, I found several things of interest. There was an unsigned love letter from an old beau that said, 'We'll be together soon,' a postcard from someone in Los Angeles saying it was nice having you around, an old letter of thanks from the Human Services Agency of San Francisco, and a couple of photos of a newborn who I assumed was a niece or nephew. I thought nothing of them at the time."

She continued to stare at me, emotionless.

"Now, you said you took a year off from Mr. McCall's employment to go home to Scandinavia for some personal matter. Is that correct?"

She said nothing.

"I know from a police investigation into your background that you don't have immigration papers, so you're an illegal alien here."

McCall looked surprised.

"Quite simply, if you left this country, more than likely, you would not be let back in without those papers," I said. "So I propose to you that the year you took off, you did not go home to Scandinavia. In fact, you didn't leave the U.S. You didn't even leave California. You went to Los Angeles to stay with a family member or friend there. Their postcard in your drawer documents that."

Svenson remained poker-faced, still in Spezzo's grip.

"But why, Ms. Svenson? Why did you take a year off to go and stay with somebody in Los Angeles and tell everyone you were going home to Scandinavia? What was the big secret?"

There was no answer from her.

"I admit that, at first, I didn't know. Those little bits of evidence I had previously mentioned, I simply wrote off. Even up to the moment that you gave yourself away, I really had no idea. But now, it all seems to fit together.

"As I said, I found it odd the way you look at Mr. McCall. It's not the normal look of an employee admiring an employer. I also found it quite strange how badly you took Johnny Spezzo's death—so much so that you needed to take some time off, and have not been the same since."

Svenson, now sitting down on a couch, just stared into her lap. McCall looked nervous.

"When I asked you about Mrs. McCall, you abruptly brushed me off. That was weird," I said. "The looks of disdain and longing, the love letter from an old beau, and the photo of a newborn all seemed connected somehow, but I couldn't quite figure out how. Not until Detective Gold told me that some pamphlets from adoption agencies were found in the glove compartment of Johnny Spezzo's car that an idea started to gel. At first, I thought that, assuming Johnny and Emily would marry, perhaps one of them was infertile and they were thinking of adopting."

I asked Emily if that was the case. She shook her head.

"Therefore, I have to ask you, Ms. Svenson: Was that old beau Mr. McCall? Were you and he having an affair?" I said, quite bluntly.

A collective gasp filled the room.

"That's enough, Robins!" said McCall. "How dare you suggest such a preposterous thing, you jackass!"

"Is it? Is it so preposterous, Ms. Svenson?" I said, pointing at her and ignoring him. "Were you, are you, not in love with Mr. McCall?"

She just sat there, looking smug.

"Did he not promise in that love letter that you would be together at some point?" I said.

No answer!

At this point, McCall lost complete control and came at me, ready to kill. I put my hands up in front of me as Ralph Wader intercepted him and held him back.

"Get out of my house!" McCall screamed. "Get out of my house!"

"That's why you stared at Mr. McCall, and why you were reluctant to discuss Mrs. McCall," I said to Svenson nervously. "You were in love with him, and she stood in your way!"

Nothing from her!

"And the reason you had to go away for a year and lied about where you were going was that you became pregnant with his love child."

"Holy crap!" I heard somebody in the group exclaim. I couldn't tell who said it.

"You wanted that baby, but you didn't want McCall to know about it at the time, because that would destroy everything."

Svenson's silence continued.

"The photos of a newborn in your dresser drawer are not of a niece or nephew at all, but of *that* child. Isn't that so, Ms. Svenson? Isn't it?"

McCall was now livid, and it was all Wader could do to contain him.

"That's why you were so devastated by the death of Johnny Spezzo— because *he* was that child, adopted shortly after birth by Sam and Lucy," I said.

An even larger collective gasp rung out.

Svenson just sat there, playing her role perfectly. Frankly, it was unnerving watching her exhibit no emotion whatsoever. I needed to do something here to get a reaction, but what?

Then it hit me. I went over to my bag and pulled out a document I had brought along. It was a copy of my father's death certificate. I made sure no one, especially Wader, a lawyer, could actually see what it was and identify it, but from a distance, the paper simply looked like something legal. And as long as no one could see it, it could be any officially notarized document.

"Ms. Svenson, I have here a legal affidavit from the Human Services Agency of San Francisco," I said.

Now Svenson started to look nervous. I opened up the document.

"'We, the Principals of the Human Services Agency of San Francisco ...'"

Svenson changed positions in her seat, looking uncomfortable.

"'... do declare that Ursula Svenson of Napa, California ...'"

Sweat formed on her brow.

"'... did willingly and legally give up for adoption ...'"

She began to tremble.

"'... a two week old baby boy, on—'"

"Yes, yes, yes, he was my son," said Svenson, "and James was the father!"

Holy crap, I was right? I just about fell over. Thank God I didn't have to proceed with my charade, because I didn't know what else I would say. I had been making it all up as I went along.

CHAPTER 34

venson collapsed back into her chair, altogether defeated. No tears—she just stared down into her lap with a lost look on her face. Emily and Denise, looking completely shocked, stared at their father with outright disgust. Emily in particular looked crazed. Even sedated somewhat, the concept that she had been sleeping with her own half-brother totally blew her away. One can only imagine the consequences had they actually married, and more so, had they produced children.

The Spezzos stared at McCall with their mouths open down around their feet.

The next few minutes were filled with confusion, screaming, and much tumult. McCall cried, and kept repeating to himself, "I had a son. I had a son." He was comforted by Ralph Wader. The Spezzos held each other for support, shooting daggers at McCall. Emily wept, and Denise just continued to stare at her father with disgust. There was chatter among the other attendees.

When things finally quieted down somewhat, I spoke.

"Johnny was adopted. Was he not, Mr. and Mrs. Spezzo?" I said, putting my father's death certificate back in my bag and looking over in their direction.

They both nodded.

"Do you mind telling me how you just happened to adopt Ms. Svenson and Mr. McCall's love child? That's beyond coincidence."

Sam Spezzo took a minute to gain some semblance of control. "When Ursula became pregnant," he said, "she approached us with her pregnancy. At first, we were entirely disgusted with her—how she could go out and become pregnant out of wedlock. She said she hadn't told the father because he was a married man, and she wouldn't tell us who he was. She said she couldn't bear to give up the child for adoption to someone and never see it again. We knew that James would fire her if he found out she was going to have a baby. We had been thinking, at the time, of having another one ourselves, so she begged, and managed to convince us, to adopt the boy as our own, so she could be close and watch him grow up. We had no idea James was the father. How could you?" he said, directing his comment at McCall and glaring at him. "God, what have we done?" He put his head down in his hands as the realization began to torment him. His wife comforted him.

"Did you ever tell Johnny he was adopted?" I said.

Without removing his hands from his face, Sam just shook his head.

"I believe he found out somehow, and wanted to seek out his birth mother," I said. "That's why he had the adoption agency pamphlets in his car. He was looking into it. And that leads me to the reason why you stole the wine, Ms. Svenson."

I turned my attention back to her.

"I don't believe you planned it at first. You waited all these years for Mr. McCall to be with you, and that's when I presume you might have told him about Johnny. The untimely death of his wife provided that opportunity, but alas, the hookup didn't materialize. Yes, you were resentful. I suppose you wanted revenge somehow, but you still loved him and couldn't bring yourself to get back at him—at least not until you were threatened!"

Looking over at her, she seemed to be in shock, just staring off into space.

"Someone who obviously needed a lot of money in a hurry approached you. They knew about your affair, the love child, and the father, and would tell Mr. McCall all about his illegitimate son if you didn't agree to help steal that rare, valuable wine. Since you knew everything about the house and Mr. McCall's wines, you were the ideal person to steal it. Although you surely didn't like being blackmailed, I suppose you saw it as an opportunity to get back at him."

She continued sitting there on the couch with her hands in her lap, staring off into oblivion.

"So, who was that person, Ms. Svenson?" I said, staring at her. "Someone so desperate, all they could think about was getting money, maybe to pay back a debt—because their life was being threatened if they didn't!"

I looked around the room, as did everyone else.

"Someone who, after being unable to easily sell that wine, began to get really desperate. Someone who went to an auction house to try and unload it!" I said.

I continued to pan the room. The others did, too.

"Someone who, when the guy at the auction house phoned to tell me about it and perhaps reveal their identity, lashed out and killed him!" I said. "Someone named . . . Horace Botner."

A hush filled the room as my eyes came to rest on Patricia.

However, I knew damn well that this theory had several flaws. First, Emily had said that she didn't think her uncle had the wits to pull off something like a theft, and I tended to agree with her. Second, Horace was pretty much bald, so a dark brown strand of hair from his head found on the body of Mr. Philips seemed highly unlikely. Finally, and more importantly, he was in the hospital in a coma at the time of the murder and obviously couldn't have done it. Even Ralph Wader commented on this fact.

"Quite right, sir," I said. "So who was it? Probably someone who cared for him, even though he was a boob—someone who loved him in spite of his making life miserable."

Patricia suddenly seemed extremely uncomfortable, fidgety and pale.

"Someone who is left-handed and dark brown-haired!"

"What are you looking at me for?" Patricia said.

I picked up a piece of paper and crumpled it up into a ball. "Catch," I said, tossing it to her.

Unconsciously reaching out, Patricia grabbed it. Looking down at the crumpled paper in her left hand, she realized what she had done and nervously said, "That doesn't mean anything. I'll bet there are other people in this room who are left-handed."

Catching the crumpled-up piece of paper in her left hand in itself wasn't sufficient evidence of guilt, and she was probably right about others in the room being left-handed. However, she started to perspire.

"I also have auburn hair, not dark brown," she said.

"Yes, that's true," I said. "However, when I was over at your place the day Horace fell into the pool and used your bathroom to change into the robe you provided, I noticed a brush with strands of dark brown hair. Now, since you have auburn hair, and Horace virtually none at all, I assumed it was your housekeeper's, but you informed me that you had let her go because you could no longer afford her. And you wouldn't keep someone else's hairbrush around, especially with their hair still on it. Therefore, I can only assume you own a dark brown wig made from real hair. Is that correct, Patricia?"

She gave no answer.

"Is that a fact, Patricia?" I said again.

Still no answer!

"Why don't you leave her alone?!" shouted Mrs. Wader, who had been silent up until now. "Hasn't she been through enough with Horace?"

I ignored her. "Patricia, do you own a dark brown-haired wig?"

Again, nothing!

"Do you own a brown-haired wig?!" I yelled.

That did it. Looking around the room and starting to tremble, she put her hands up to her face and broke down, wailing.

"I didn't mean to kill him!" she cried. "I didn't mean it."

Denise ran over to Patricia, swept her up in her arms, and coddled her, telling her everything would be fine.

Turning back to me, Patricia said, "They were going to kill him if I didn't pay. My sweet Horace! They were going to kill him."

She bawled like a baby.

After several minutes more, Wader stepped up. "Aren't you forgetting something?" he said.

I looked at him with a puzzled expression on my face as I dabbed my forehead with a tissue.

"The wine—where is it now, then?" he said.

I stuffed the tissue in my shirt pocket. "I'll bet my bottom dollar it's somewhere in that passageway," I said.

With that statement, hushed whispering and mumbling could be heard around the room.

As that revelation sank into the gathered throng, something bothered me about Patricia. "Why didn't you simply ask your brother for help?" I said.

Between sobs, she said, "James had helped me out several times before, but wouldn't do so again. He said he couldn't keep bailing me out. The problem needed to be corrected once and for all."

With that, I went over to the window, pulled the curtain apart, and signaled Georgey and his officers to come in. He and four officers entered the room. I took him aside for a moment and told him the details. He did the rest, taking into custody those who needed to be taken.

Trembling, I went over to the bar and poured myself a good, stiff shot of Maker's Mark bourbon, and downed it in one shot. I was exhausted, depleted, and, frankly, surprised and shocked that I had pulled this off. If the truth be known, I was quite proud of myself. I had managed to solve the case, most of it without the evidence I had on my tape recorder.

I left Georgey and his men to do their thing. As I grabbed my bag to go, Wader came over and interrupted me.

"One thing still puzzles me," he said. "You said that someone deliberately infected the security system's computer with a virus. Who did it? Was it Ms. Svenson?"

"A good question, sir. And even though she orchestrated and stole the wine, I don't believe she's computer-savvy enough to do something like that. You yourself swore that a swarthy-looking chap was once out from the security company to examine the vault security system. McCall verified that a guy once came out. However, Joey Touchstone, who created the system, emphasized that she was the only person who maintained her systems.

"So my guess is that Ms. Svenson got her own computer specialist—a guy, obtained through Lambeck and his mob connections, pretending to be from Touchstone. The premise was making some adjustments, but in fact, it was to infect the vault computer with the virus. Mr. McCall was there, standing over the guy the whole time, as you said that day in your office, and since the guy said Joey was sick, McCall had no reason to suspect anything."

Wader nodded as I turned to leave.

"One more thing, Woody!" he said.

"Yes?" I said, turning back to him.

"May I take a look at that affidavit?"

I just smiled.

He looked at me funny for a moment. Then, realizing what I had done, a smile came to his face.

"Very clever," he said.

I glanced over at McCall, who was crumpled up in one of the easy chairs, looking completely destroyed. As much as I didn't like the man, I couldn't help but feel sorry for him.

Hopping into my car, I headed home. En route, I called Sadie to see how things were with her and Julia. I told her that the case was solved, and it was probably safe now for Julia to return to her apartment. With no further direction from Svenson, the thugs she hired to rough her up would probably not do anything else. As a precaution, though, I would urge Georgey to keep an officer on guard at her place for a few more days.

As I drove along, I felt as if a huge weight had been lifted from my shoulders. It had been quite the evening.

CHAPTER 35

On Tuesday about noon, I received a call from Ralph Wader telling me they had found the wine in the passageway. He also said McCall wanted me to send Wader an invoice so McCall could cut a check promptly.

"Is the wine back in the vault?" I said.

Wader informed me it was.

"You know, Ralph, I've never actually seen that Chambertin in person," I said. "Would it be possible to come by and take a look at it? You know, to make sure it's okay and not damaged from its adventure."

He thought about it for a moment.

"Well, I suppose so, but Mr. McCall won't see you, or anyone," Wader said. "He gave me strict instructions."

"I understand." I really didn't want to see McCall anyway.

Wader said he would meet me at the house around 3 p.m. and show me the wine. I then drew up my invoice and e-mailed it to Wader.

It was a hot day, and before heading out to the estate, I went into the kitchen to get a cold drink. Pouring myself a glass of orange juice, I opened the freezer to get some ice.

"What the hell!" I said, stepping back.

Sitting there, staring back at me, was my stupid tape recorder. How on earth it got in the freezer, I had no idea. I must have gone in there with the machine in hand and put it down to get something inside, then completely forgot about it. To think that I was making myself crazy looking for the damn thing, when the whole time it was almost under my nose. I had to laugh.

I tried to play it, but it was too frozen to work. Placing it on my office desk, I hoped it would be okay once it thawed out.

When I got to the house, Ralph Wader answered the door. There was nobody else around. He informed me that Patricia, Svenson, and Lambeck were in custody. Detective Gold had already told me that Lambeck was a wanted man in New York, and maybe that was why he was hiding out here on the west coast—to avoid the authorities. But why play an English butler? Perhaps because he was a two-bit actor and somehow saw it as an intriguing role, or more likely, because it was all part of a plan to steal something from McCall—and not necessarily wine. After all, McCall is a man with quite a few valuable items in his possession. This might also explain why Lambeck's mob buddies were out here, too. Maybe this is what Svenson found out, and she used it to get Lambeck's help with the thugs.

Whether Georgey was going to pursue the mobsters involved, other than the guy they apprehended trying to snuff me out in the hospital, he didn't know.

Lambeck, Amos, and Svenson had all lost their jobs. Emily was in terrible shape, and Denise had left to stay with a friend for a while.

I asked how Horace was doing, and Wader told me he was still in a coma, but the doctors seemed more positive about him possibly coming out of it. I wondered what would become of him if Patricia went to prison. I also pondered what would happen to Denise and Amos as a couple now that Amos was no longer employed by McCall. The state of McCall's relationship with the Spezzos after this, I couldn't even speculate about. And as for the relationship between McCall and his daughters, especially after finding out that he had played around on their mother and fathered a child in the process, I could only imagine things would be far worse than they already were.

As Wader led me downstairs to the game room with the vault, he handed me an envelope. I opened it to find a check for far more than I'd asked for, and it included that extremely large "finder's" fee. *Wonderful! Now Sadie can get her operation!* I thought. Somehow, I half-expected a note of some sort from McCall along with the payment, but there was none.

I pocketed the check as Wader flipped the secret panel on the bar, revealing the returned wine on the monitor. He then entered the code to open the vault door, allowing me to enter. I went in.

And there it was, looking magnificent: a double magnum of 1784 Chambertin with Napoleon's initials etched into the glass, just as in the photo. I took out a magnifying glass I had brought with me. I perused every inch of the bottle from top to bottom for its detail. Usually, this kind of rare, historical artifact is hermetically sealed under glass, inaccessible to the public.

Moving the magnifying glass over the treasure, it didn't appear its recent escapade had harmed it any, but I really had nothing to go by other than the photo. I carefully noted Napoleon's coat of arms and looked for some indication as to who the producer might be, but found none. Maybe it was its supposed curse, or maybe it was my mind playing tricks on me, but there was a strange, eerie air in the vault.

As I closely studied the bottom label, with the words "Le Chambertin," something caught my eye. *Wait a minute*, I thought. *That doesn't make any sense.*

Rubbing my eyes, I re-examined the label. It didn't look right. To the best of my knowledge, printing back in the late eighteenth century was quite primitive, and any kind of ink would run a bit over time. However, the print on this label was totally intact. In fact, it looked like the lettering had been burned into the label and filled with ink.

There is only one way to get that kind of clean finish when printing, and that is with a laser printer.

I'm no historian, but I could pretty much bet my life on the fact that laser printers were not around back in the 1780s.

I jolted upright in astonishment.

Holy moly, it's a fake.

Did McCall know it was a fake? Had he purchased it not knowing? Did the previous owner know?

Then, it hit me: When Philips examined the wine for authenticity at the auction house, he must have noticed the discrepancy. That's probably why he wanted me to come right over. The guy was just as flabbergasted as I.

My guess is that Philips told Patricia. She must have become so enraged to learn that the wine she had conspired to steal from her own brother was worthless, she went nuts. Then, when Philips tried to call me to tell me about it and possibly divulge her identity, she lashed out and hit him with the bung mallet. She probably never meant to kill him, just as she had said.

Christopher Columbus!

When the shock of my discovery finally subsided, I found myself facing a moral dilemma—should I inform Wader and McCall about the wine or not? Coming out of the vault, I signaled Wader to close it up. As we made our way back upstairs, I wrestled with the decision. By the time we were back at the front door, my mind was made up.

I directed my 'Vette out of Carneros and onto the highway, San Francisco-bound, without speaking to Wader or McCall. Why?

First of all, McCall didn't want to speak to anyone. In the last twenty-four hours, the poor man had lost a housekeeper, butler, chauffeur, and possibly good friends, the Spezzos. He was on the outs with his two daughters, not to mention his sister, and who knew if those relationships would ever be mended? In the last short while, he had also lost a son, although previously unknown to him, and less than a year earlier, he had lost his wife. Really, what did he have left?

That wine! It had come to mean so much to him. I wasn't fond of the man, but I simply did not have the heart to take that away from him.

Call it immoral. Call it unethical. I don't care. Besides, the chances of that wine being stolen again were a million to one, and if everyone, including the insurance company, thought it was legit, then who exactly was it hurting? No one!

Now, as to whether Patricia someday says otherwise, I cannot say, but the truth would never come from me.

As I drove home, there were a couple things I wondered about. Did the fact that the wine was made from Pinot Noir and not, say, Cabernet, Shiraz, or any other varietal cast a spell of sorts over the players? Why pose such a question, you might ask?

Well, there is a certain magic that is Pinot. You remember how McCall talked about it when we first met. It was as if he was possessed. "I'm absolutely mad about Pinot Noir," he had said. "That's why I became a grape-grower."

Or was it the so-called curse? Pendry had said that there had been much misfortune and many deaths associated with the wine throughout its history. God knows there was certainly a fair share here.

By the time I got home and let Mouton out into the yard for some fresh air, it was time to get ready for a dinner date with Julia. I didn't know if we would get back together or not. Nothing had actually changed, or at least we hadn't talked about it. When she came to see me in the hospital, she was warm and loving. Should I have taken that as a sign that we were back together? I didn't know. But she had at least agreed to go to dinner with me.

I donned a pair of light cotton, pleated, sand colored slacks, a wine-colored collarless shirt, black suspenders, and dark Italian leather loafers. Upon my noggin was a gray felt fedora with a wide brim and burgundy-colored band.

Preparing to leave, I gazed at myself in the hall mirror. "Belissima!" I cried, kissing my fingers the way the Italians do when something tastes good. I looked like Bogey from *The Maltese Falcon*. I could live with that.

I motored to Julia's place, and within a couple minutes, she appeared, looking radiant. Garbed in a short, black dress, matching heels, and leather clutch bag, she took my breath away.

"Hello," she said, climbing into the car and giving me a peck on the cheek. "Where are we going?"

"Boulevard," I said.

As we headed to the restaurant, I wondered about our relationship, if we had one. Personally speaking, I was a changed man. All that had gone down with the McCalls had made me realize how misguided my thinking about relationships had been. Observing those between Emily, Denise, and their father, between Emily and Johnny, between Denise and Amos, and between Patricia and Horace really enlightened me. They were all flawed. None was perfect. Yet these people all indulged and moved forward, regardless of the consequences—even death. The sacrifices Patricia had made for love, even if taken in a horrible direction, showed me its power. What was I afraid of?

I really did love Julia, and seeing her in danger emphasized that. And just because most of the relationships I had seen growing up were dismal didn't necessarily mean ours would be. We had a good thing going, and not wanting to live together for fear of what negative things might happen didn't seem to make much sense. It was not a way to live my life. Love's a gamble, and there are no guarantees, but it's every bit worth the bet. Come what may, I was ready to commit. And after almost getting killed myself, the idea of living with my girlfriend seemed like a piece of cake.

It didn't scare me anymore.

Just before we got out of the car at the restaurant, I pulled something out of my jacket pocket.

"I got you something," I said, handing it to her.

"What's this?" she said, looking puzzled as she took it from me.

"It's a change of address card."

"But I haven't found a place yet," she said, confused.

"I took the liberty of filling it out for you."

Reading the card very carefully, she said, "But that's your address."

"I know."

"I don't understand," she said, looking even more bewildered. Then the light went on. She looked down at the card again and back at me. A smile that could light up the darkest night danced across her face.

"Oh, yes. Yes, I will. I love you, Woody."

That's what I wanted to hear.

She threw her arms around me and kissed me passionately.

As we got out of the car and walked around to the entrance, I was reminded of an old saying: "He who laughs last probably didn't get the joke initially." I'm not exactly sure why that particular line came to mind, or what it meant, but for the moment, the woman I loved was by my side, my dear aunt would be able to get her much-needed operation, and life was good.

"Woody, I understand this restaurant has an absolutely fabulous wine list, with an amazing Burgundy selection. Maybe we can order a Chambertin," Julia said, chuckling slightly.

I gave her a dirty look.

"What's the matter? You're not afraid of a little Pinot, are you? It might be cursed." She laughed.

I simply smirked. *Who knows? Anything is possible.*

ACKNOWLEDGEMENTS

Words of gratitude are extremely important. By verbally expressing those thoughts, the people who help and inspire us along the way get the recognition they deserve. Because of their contributions, the road to our ultimate goal is a lot less bumpy. Here's to those who made my road smoother.

Thanks to friends and colleagues, Tony Aspler and Gord Stimmell: Tony, whose entertaining fictional wine books motivated me to plunge into the world of fantasy; and Gord, whose down-to-earth style of wine writing have always enlightened me.

Praise to the California Wine Institute for being a beacon of knowledge, providing me endless information in the creation of this work.

Kudos to *Wine Spectator*, *Decanter*, and *Wine Enthusiast* magazines for offering up endless ideas for storylines.

My sincere appreciation goes to Bruce Bortz and Bancroft Press, who took a leap of faith to publish my story.

Very special thanks to my brilliant editor, Harrison Demchick, who taught me much and without whose guidance, direction, and expertise this book would not have come to fruition.

A heartfelt tip of the hat to Ravenshoe Group for all its hard work and creative input into potential cover designs.

Last, but definitely not least, I am indebted to my good friends Rick and Linda Wigmore, whose generous support and input into the content have proved invaluable.

One final note of recognition: to Pinot lovers everywhere. Without you and your crazy fascination for this spellbinding grape, this story would never have been told.

RAVENSHOE GROUP

ABOUT THE AUTHOR

E dward Finstein, aka "The Wine Doctor," is an internationally recognized wine expert. He is the award-winning author of the reference book *Ask the Wine Doctor*.

A TV and radio host, he is a renowned journalist writing for numerous newspapers, magazines and on the Internet in North America and abroad.

As an international wine judge, he travels the world judging in competitions.

Edward is also a Professor of Wine at George Brown College's School of Hospitality and Culinary Arts, a wine consultant, wine appraiser, wine tour guide, and former V.P. of the Wine Writers' Circle of Canada.

"Doc," as he is known, believes wine should be fun, and he preaches the gospel with a sense of humor and whimsy.

He lives in Toronto with his wife Jo Ann and their cat Pepper.

You can reach him through his website www.winedoctor.ca or via email at winedoctor@sympatico.ca.